First published in 2017
by Dodo Ink, an imprint of
Dodo Publishing Co Ltd
Flat 5, 21 Silverlands, Buxton SK17 6QH
www.dodoink.com

The right of James Miller to be identified as the author of this work
has been asserted in accordancewith Section 77 of the Copyright,
Designs and Patents Act 1988

This is a work of fiction. Names, characters, places and incidents
are either the product of the author's imagination or are used
fictitiously, and any resemblance to actual persons, living or dead, or
actual events or locales is entirely coincidental.

An earlier version of *Eat My Face* was published in Issue VII of
Paraphilia Magazine (2011). An earlier version of *Hope's End* was
published in the anthology *A Dream of Stone* (Apophenia, 2013).
Exploding Zombie Cock was originally published as a Galley Beggar
Singles Club eBook (2014).

A CIP record for this book
is available from the British Library

Cover design: Joe Wilson
Copyeditor: Jayne White
Typesetter: Ben Ottridge

ISBN 978-0-9935758-5-3 paperback

Printed and bound in Great Britain by TJ International Trecerus
Industrial Estate, Padstow, Cornwall PL28 8RW.

UNAMERICAN ACTIVITIES

JAMES MILLER

CONTENTS

UNPROLOGUE

The origins of the collection you are about to read go back to the summer of 2010, a complicated time for me. In the space of a few weeks I published my second novel *Sunshine State*, split up with my then girlfriend (or, to be more accurate, she left me) and was offered a job due to start in the autumn. This combination of circumstances conspired to make me feel both more and less secure than ever before. On the one hand I was confident that I was on the 'right path' as people call it and that after years spent writing, studying and teaching I was finally being recognised, if not with literary 'fame' then at least a permanent post at a decent university and a glimmer of what might be called 'financial security'.

But alongside these positive developments I was assailed with pangs of dread, moments of horror and emptiness when I was certain that – far from taking the 'right path' – I had found myself in a situation where everything was very wrong, as if I had finally passed through into a parallel universe of continuous unease where I could no longer be quite sure of anything and when it seemed as if the things I had could be taken away in an instant, my (ex-) girlfriend's sudden departure a sign for other, more totalising, destabilising developments to come.

During this period, I was living in south London, in a tower block overlooking the Elephant and Castle roundabout. The lease was due to expire in six weeks' time and I lingered on alone in the small apartment stripped of most of its possessions (which had belonged to the ex-girlfriend), overwhelmed with a self-lacerating paralysis, as if the wreckage from which I surveyed myself was a way of saying, 'here it is, here's the catastrophe you always knew was coming, it's here, you dickhead!' (But we know that the great catastrophe, like all great catastrophes, is still to come.) The apartment faced the constant grime and grind of the roundabout and had tall, double-glazed windows that were impossible to open very wide and were covered by ill-fitting drapes. In the afternoon sun the apartment would heat up like a greenhouse and I would lie sweating on the sofa wearing only my underpants, trying desperately to cool things down with a single desk fan, waiting for the sun to dip, waiting for darkness to bring a chill to the flat, windows rattling and banging if there was a breeze, all of it giving me the sensation that I lived on a mountain, a place of extremes, like a hermit or one of those holy men – anchorites – who make their abode in small cells on the side of great cliff walls. I would look down at the roundabout watching cyclists negotiate the traffic. The roundabout is a notorious 'accident blackspot' and every few weeks one of them would be pulled under a lorry or a bus with the result that bouquets of bedraggled flowers, laminated photographs of victims and handwritten tributes would adorn the streetlamps and crash barriers, small shrines to the dead that seemed more suited, perhaps, to a Mexican barrio or Neapolitan backstreets than central London.

I was quite alone and spent many, many days not talking to a soul, pacing the streets, anxious, tearful and filled with gloom: I had made – as I saw it then – another miscalculation. Although certain that new experiences still awaited me (I was only thirty-four, not old, not by any measure), I struggled to shake the feeling that it was all over and that everything still to happen would only be a hollow repetition or echo of what had been. Of course, looking back, it's all quite ridiculous and yet, also true. But when one is alone for long periods, morbid thoughts tend to accumulate.

In other ways, I was shocked to realise life had moved on with startling speed: all my old friends from university were married with small children, pragmatically banished to the outer suburbs with little time left to offer comfort or companionship and anyway I could hardly blame them. Writing and the ex-girlfriend had consumed almost all of my time but if I'm honest that's just an excuse as I was never very sociable anyway. No, the only person to blame for my solitude was me. Fact is, I didn't particularly want to see anyone in case the measure of bourgeois comfort my old friends had achieved (houses, cars, savings, pension schemes) served only to show me how by choosing what might be called the 'literary life' I had in fact chosen nothing at all.

One day, as all this was happening, I received my first email from 'Tim'. I'm calling him 'Tim' so you know it's not his real name. The email arrived around nine or ten in the morning with the subject SUNSHINE STATE FACTUAL ERRORS as I was busy smoking my first or second joint of the day and drinking my second or third coffee. My first thought, when I saw the email, was 'oh no' but it was a muted, dull sort of 'oh no' as if my second novel didn't really have anything to do with me. Reactions to *Sunshine State* had been muted; a bad review in one broadsheet, a lukewarm review in another and a good one in a cool magazine that nobody read for book reviews. That was about it. My Amazon sales ranking peaked briefly around the three thousand mark and then went into a steady decline. As a result, the novelty of receiving an email about it from an actual reader was more than enough to provoke my curiosity. The email was scrupulously polite, if a little long-winded. 'Dear James Miller,' Tim began, 'I read with great interest your novel *Sunshine State* partly because I was, until not so long ago, a resident of Miami and it's true, what you suggest, one day the sea will rise up and swallow this great city, everyone knows it even if no one will admit it.' After saying a few nice things about the book, Tim went on to point out a number of minor factual errors and inaccuracies, references to 'petrol' rather than 'gas' and so on, nothing major. I contemplated forwarding his email to the copy-editor, then decided against it. I wasn't even sure how much I cared.

I was more curious to know how Tim had come across a copy as it hadn't been published in the United States. Perhaps an indie bookshop had ordered a few on import? All the same, I was having a bad morning and after the third joint I forgot all about the email and went back to bed to sob uncontrollably until lunchtime when hunger finally displaced my grief and, fortified with another joint, I stumbled down to the Nandos restaurant located underneath my block. I ate almost nothing but Nandos that summer.

A few days later I received a second email from Tim. Again, it was scrupulously polite and apologised at length for the previous email and for having the 'temerity' to point out a few 'inconsequential errors' when I was after all 'a published author' and he was 'not'. Tim went on in this fashion spinning a slightly desperate story about how he also aspired to write and had, in fact, written quite a lot. He was, he said, a writer 'of sorts' but in recent years had been 'very unsettled'. 'I am,' he emailed, 'once again on the road. It's often this way.' He alluded to his work as being what he called 'unsuitable for publication' hinting that it was not something with which his name could be associated. It was a long email and I struggle to remember much about it now, but I do recall it was troubled. This man is troubled, I thought to myself. But I was also 'troubled' and so having nothing better to do I decided to reply, thanking Tim for his messages and asking if there was anything I could do to 'help him out', a decision that has since had a number of consequences.

The next few days were the same as the last. I mentioned that I saw little of my old friends during this time but I did, however, have one friend who was going through a bitter divorce, an experience infinitely worse than my own break-up. I had lost very little, but my friend's ex-wife had taken his children back to America, forced him to sell his house and was now suing for his trust fund. As a result his doctor had prescribed tranquilisers – Valium – to help him cope with the stress and so whenever we met he would drop a pill into my hand and thus immunised we would set forth together, drifting from pub to bar to club ostensibly to 'meet women'. Of course we never met anybody or even spoke to anyone and I was usually so drunk when I got home that I was sick while the brutal hangover the next day meant that a few Valium, kept in reserve for such occasions, and many, many spliffs were necessary to take the edge off it all. It was a confusing time. One evening, as all this was happening, Tim emailed me again.

Before we go any further I should add that some time ago there was a problem with my email account. I think it was hacked. I'm not sure. Emails disappeared, that sort of thing. Now I have a different account and access to the old account has been lost, the saved messages, years of correspondence between me and friends and girlfriends and whatever cast into cyberspace oblivion. I suppose I should also admit that I'm recreating this from a rather hazy memory of what I remember reading almost seven years ago now, but I do remember that Tim's life, at least as far as he represented himself to me, was a complicated affair. He told me all this in various emails and in a single long phone conversation. I only spoke to him once, late at night. Tim, I remember, had a voice that struck me as up-tight and laid-back at the same time. I pictured him first a bit like the Dude in *The Big Lebowski* and then as a David Foster Wallace type of neurotic American geek-genius sweating into his bandana whilst writing away on the same sort of typewriter Hemingway might have used.

But all this is stupid.

The point is I didn't get a very clear impression and I don't like talking on the phone. As we spoke I was desperate for the conversation to end but was too polite to cut him off. He had a lot to say. He was, as I mentioned, a 'troubled' man. I gathered that he came from what he referred to as an 'illustrious' family in Washington DC. His grandfather had been a senator and his father was also influential, but dead – died mysteriously, Tim explained – with twelve other government men when their aeroplane went down over Oklahoma in a 'freak tornado' or some such uniquely American disaster. Since then, Tim said he had cut himself loose from all that. He mentioned various types of casual, manual work, hanging out with Mexican labourers and Alaskan fishermen, an MFA in creative writing, trouble with the law and 'substance abuse issues'. Perhaps there was family money in the picture, a little something to keep him afloat, I don't know. He wasn't young, that's the other thing, don't think of him as a young man. No, he was more like forty, perhaps fifty. He was older, had lived a bit and suffered much. Or perhaps that should be suffered a bit and lived much, something like that. It seems to me that after a while the two become synonymous.

Anyway, one of these emails came attached with a few stories and more apologies as he asked me to read them but only if I felt like it. He said they were 'rough' and in need of 'polish' but expressed a desire for me to help him publish them. 'These are my un-American activities,' he wrote.

Afterwards events became more disordered. The lease on the flat expired and I was embroiled in some sort of protracted argument with the landlord who seemed determined to keep the entire deposit as compensation for a tiny crack in the bathroom floor. Rents were soaring and I found myself, despite the new job, priced out of the market. As a result, I was forced back to live with my parents, returning (the ultimate failure) to the same bedroom where I had spent my lonely and frustrated teenage years. I was commuting three hours a day to my job at the university and had little time to think about Tim. After some months of argument, I threatened to take the landlord to arbitration and he capitulated, returning the deposit minus a hundred pounds. Towards Christmas I found a flat share in Stockwell. The rent consumed 70% of my salary. Perhaps things were looking up, perhaps I was back on the 'right path'? It's hard to say.

At some point, while this was happening, I had a look at what Tim called his 'stories'. They were interesting, by which I mean they pulled me in, had moments of daring and made me laugh. But they were very rough, like first drafts, with the air of being written on the hoof, some mere fragments or sketches or obscene rants and I struggled to know what to make of it all, if what I was reading was an elaborate joke or deadly serious or perhaps both. There was crazy stuff about vampires and aliens, porn-stars and meth-addicts, secret conspiracies to rule the world and dark secrets buried in the earth. Was it genre fiction, satire or some strange hybrid of both? I didn't really understand why Tim had sent them to me. What was I meant to say? What did he think I could do? I might have been a 'published author' but I was also a nobody, with few contacts and minimal influence over anything. There seemed no real reason other than that he must have been another lonely, desperate guy reaching out to someone (anyone). Christ, there are millions like him, like me. 'These are great,' I think I emailed back. 'So funny.'

All I can say is that just before Christmas I had a final email from Tim. I'd never received an email quite like it (and I've never received one since). It came late at night as I was sprawled out on the sofa watching *South Park* and thinking about bed. We'd had a lot of snow, unusual for London in December, snow and bitter storms and I'd hurt my back after doing something foolish with an old television. Anyway, I wasn't sure what to make of the email. As I said, the original is lost but I recall Tim saying that he was in 'great danger' and that he had uncovered something 'terrible' and as a result this would be the 'last I would ever hear from him'. He also wrote 'The truth is in these stories', and I think he may have finished the email with 'by the time you receive this, I will most likely be dead'. Was he really in danger or was it all just attention-seeking melodrama? Perhaps I should have sent him more feedback? I felt suddenly very guilty. Anyway, amid these doomy warnings he told me I could do as I liked with his stories. Rewrite them, change them, polish them, delete them, 'I don't care.' That was all. I seem to remember a symbolic boom of thunder, as if to give his email an appropriately dramatic undertone, but I'm sure that's an invention of my memory. I fretted a bit, tried to compose a reply but failed. It was late, I was tired and my back was hurting. I figured I'd send a proper reply in the morning but I never got around to it.

So Tim, I'm sorry about that. I've emailed you since to tell you about the stories and see if you like what I've done with them but the emails came back as address unknown. I googled you a few times but Google had no answers. I guess maybe you are dead now, perhaps they 'got you', who knows? In the end I hope I came good or at least did a little of what was wanted. Here are the stories. I changed every word. Make of them as you will.

EAT MY FACE

Eventually, Rick passes out and I decide it's time to go home. It's about three miles from Rick's place to mine. He promised me a lift but I'm happy to walk. The neighbourhood is deserted at this early hour, the streets free of traffic, the houses dark and getting darker, somehow, as the sky behind them slowly brightens. Downtown is always quiet at the best of times and I can't shake the feeling that I'm being watched as I pass the old town hall and department store, both abandoned for as long as I've lived here. There's no one about, not even the regular bums and winos who hang out in the park near the war memorial. I guess they must be sleeping. I duck down when I hear an approaching car – just in case it's the sheriff or one of his deputies and I don't want to answer questions when I'm high like this – but the car, whoever it was, turns away and then nothing but silence again, that and the steady hum of insects in the undergrowth. These muggy southern nights.

Not far now. As I stroll down the middle of the road I can almost pretend this is a good place. There are more trees than houses and in the misty light the imperfections are hidden – the run-down buildings, the sagging rooftops and mouldy old porches: it's easier to ignore the messed up yards, the rusting cars resting on blocks, the wood piles, the trash piles, the broken air conditioning units left out to rot, the fact that this is the sort of town most people have forgotten about, the sort of town most people leave if they can.

Even so, dawn turns the sky from deep blue to silver and for a fleeting moment I almost feel good about myself and the world, as if this is the moment of renewal, when everything starts again, when most people turn in their beds and enjoy a new dream. Funny. Funny what I think when I'm like this. I must be high as a motherfucker, still up, still buzzing, but it won't be long before I enter that grey area, neither high nor not high: I'll be in sight of the crash, like a guy on a mountain looking down at the desert he knows he's got to cross. Something like that, anyhow.

I pause, doubling up to hack and cough. Lurid green phlegm in the gutter. Urgh. Got to stop, got to cut it out, at least for a little bit. Got to. We've been hitting it hard, Rick and I, ever since he punked those dealers up in Macon. That was probably a mistake. Yeah. Well, pretty much everything is a mistake.

Home. I let myself in. Ma will be asleep and it's quiet inside, just the drip from the leaky faucet and the hmm of the refrigerator. My phone tells me it's five-thirty which means I've got to be at work in about four hours. Man, this is going to be painful. I rummage around in my room, trying not to make too much noise. I find my bud and some papers and build a small blunt to help take the edge off and hopefully knock me out. Got to stop this. Got to sleep. It's Rick's fault really. Rick was hitting it hard yesterday because he's under a lot of stress. I know, I understand.

Rick owes three thousand dollars to these meth dealers near Macon and lately they've been starting to ask when the money will come. That's where we got the crystal from, 'Pure North Korean shit' Rick says, 'Spark me up some Kim Jong Bomb' as he lights the pipe.

The other reason is that Rick's dad is due to be released from prison any day now and Rick's dad is one scary motherfucker. Could be that this problem will make the other problem go away 'cause the dealers know that to mess with Rick means to mess with Rick's dad and Rick's dad is the meanest, most cold-hearted bastard in the whole of Dooly County but then maybe not, maybe that won't happen. I don't know.

I need to lie down. Need to close my eyes.

***

Work is the McDonald's in the retail strip on the outskirts of town. LeRoi can tell I'm a mess so he puts me on the register where I stand drooling and mumbling at customers. Thankfully, we hardly have no one come in all afternoon. I'm jittering and pissing sweat through my uniform and LeRoi looks at me like I'm something he can't wait to scrape off his shoe. Finally it's time for my break and I realise I can't remember the last time I ate anything so I eat a Big Mac and then I'm sick in the toilets. The bad taste in my mouth is getting worse. I go out for a cigarette and fresh air. Out back, past the dumpsters where LeRoi says he once saw an armadillo the size of a hog there's really nothing just more parking then the pine woods. Part of me is looking at the trees, green and mysterious just wishing I could run off into them and never come back... but then I know the woods don't lead nowhere unless you call the dairy factory where Randy and Brett work somewhere and I don't, so I don't run, I don't do nothing but smoke my last three cigarettes. I really need more bud to take the edge off the meth but that will have to wait. Slow, slow, slow, everything going so slow.

Finally, the day is over but Rick is waiting for me in the parking lot.

'Hey man, I'm done in, I need to get home.'

'Bullshit, come on bro, let's go for a drive.'

'I'm finished.' But there's little use in protesting so I get in. I can tell right away Rick is high as an airship: there's that weird sort of empty light to his eyes and he's been chewing his lips so much the bottom one is split and bleeding.

'I wanna... I wanna go and visit Mom,' Rick says, so we drive out to Anderson and the spot where his mom was murdered. Rick doesn't say anything but then he doesn't need to. We've done this enough. His mom was a maid at a motel that has long since been demolished. It's just a vacant lot on the outskirts of Anderson, overgrown with weeds and wild flowers. Rick comes here, now and then, says he feels 'close' to her. Truth is a psychopath murdered his mom when she was cleaning the room. The killer hid in the bathroom then leapt out and stabbed her to death, used her blood to write weird shit about Satan on the walls, was caught, found guilty and got the chair. But all this was long ago, way before my time. Anyway, we pull up at the vacant lot and Rick lights a cigarette and looks sort of thoughtful. 'Dad's out,' he says at last.

'No shit!'

'Yeah. Well, he phoned me from a whorehouse in Birmingham and said to expect him back in the next couple of days.'

Rick was wearing his Metallica T-shirt and there was this sickly smell coming off him like meat left out to spoil.

'How was he?'

'Drunk.'

'When you last see him?'

He doesn't answer. Rick's dad was never around much even before he got put away but I remember he was never a very reassuring presence. Originally, see, I'm from upstate New York, but then we moved down here 'cause my dad changed work. This was before the crummy bastard walked out on Ma and me. When I was new at school Rick was one of the few guys who'd be friendly. We soon found out we had lots in common. We loved watching horror movies for a start. Rick's favourite was *The Texas Chainsaw Massacre*, the original one, not the bullshit remake. I liked the *Saw* movies and *The Ring*, both the American and the Japanese versions. Everyone in the school hated us but that was okay because they were a bunch of farm-boys, jocks and air-head gum-chewing bitches. Sometimes we used to talk about doing a Columbine on them all but in the end it never seemed worth it. Anyway, I don't much like hurting people. I'm no good at fighting. It's true. I always get my ass kicked. It's best to avoid that. Like Rick says, he says, 'Covey, you just a skinny puny weird looking motherfucker, don't get no ideas.' Rick's different though.

He'll get involved even if he's going to lose. Like when he took on a couple of bikers after they called him a fag then kicked several shades of shit out of him. I thought he was dead but he still managed to get up, blood gushing from this gash in his forehead. He wouldn't go to the hospital, he just sat at home with his head in a towel, a bottle of bourbon and smoked some rocks. You can still see the scar, a white line jumping up and down his forehead. Once he tried to get us to cut our wrists and share our blood, make us like brothers or something but I refused. Razors hurt and I'm squeamish. Sometimes Rick says he'd like to live forever but I always think, what for? To work in McDonald's every fucking day for eternity. Fuck that.

'It ain't like that fucking film,' he says, changing the subject.

'What?'

'The vampires.'

'What's that got to do with anything?'

'Vampires. It ain't like *Twilight*. Piece of shit film. Vegetarian vampires. What a lot of bull.'

'I know.' Rick knows I know. We're both agreed that *Twilight* is the worst film ever made.

'They run things, you do understand this, don't you?' Rick says. 'They've lived for thousands of years and they regenerate themselves when they need to. It's the original bloodline, that's the ones we need to get.'

Rick often talks like this. He's fond of vampires, very interested. Vampires, aliens, the Illuminati. All that shit. He has his theories, says there's a big difference between humans who have been made into vampires by other vampires and those who are part of the vampire race that once ruled the earth tens of thousands of years ago and who used humans as their slaves. He often seems to think something or another is running shit. If it's not the Illuminati it's vampires. Mostly vampires. Bush was a vampire. Obama's a vampire. The only president who wasn't a vampire was Clinton, ''cause vampires don't get busted for getting a blow job from an intern' as Rick is fond of saying. Vampires making war on the rest, a conflict going back ten million years to when they first crashed their spaceship on this planet and experimented on the humans they found and separated the races and created all the problems that have continued to this very day. That's what Rick says, anyway.

We smoke some more of the North Korean shit and go for another drive. The sun was setting when we went out to visit Rick's mom and now it's dark. Nightfall comes quick. We turn off the Interstate and drive some distance. A glimpse of a house set behind a high verge then we stop at the end of the drive to the mansion. An old plantation house. We pass it all the time. There have always been rumours about this place and I thought it was abandoned but not so, I discover. Rick turns off the lights and the engine and there is this weird scratching, knocking noise and it's only when Rick says, 'What's that?' that I realise it's my leg kicking against the seat. 'They're back,' says Rick.

'Who?'

'Vampires.'

'Are you crazy?'

'Come on.'

We open the doors and step out and the night is really warm. We creep up the driveway towards the mansion.

A faint mist swirls around and my whole body is shaking although I can't tell if it's the meth or something else.

'Why do you think they're vampires?'

Rick leans over, grabs my mouth. 'Just shut the fuck up!'

I push away. 'Jesus man, what the fuck?'

'Shut up and come on,' he whispers and so we creep along the driveway, gravel scrunching underfoot, the house getting closer. Under the pines to our left are several vehicles, a Chevy Suburban, a Cadillac saloon and a small Mercedes sports car, polished dark and shiny as coffins. A light is on in a front room and the curtains are open. I see some sort of chandelier and old furniture draped in white sheets.

Rick grabs my arm hard. 'I saw them taking out the coffin,' he hisses.

'What?'

'They took out the coffin and drove it to the cemetery, the one near Red Hook, in a black limo. It wasn't what you think, it wasn't that. They put him in the ground, but he's going to come back.' Agitated, he pushes his face close to mine. 'We've got to stop them!'

Through the window we see people sitting in the room, an old man, an old woman with a shock of white hair swirling like a halo. A younger woman. The young woman moves back and forth. We lean forward for a better look then Rick stumbles, grabbing me and we fall on top of each other. A security light comes on, illuminating us floundering like hogs in the dirt.

We scramble to our feet. The old man is standing by the window, pressing his face to the glass, looking out.

'Rick!'

'Just fucking run, just go, go, go.'

We jump back into the car. Rick turns us round so fast we almost go off the road, kicking up more dirt, the old Buick moaning and then he floors it and we're rocketing away. Only when we reach the Interstate do I remember to tell him to turn on the headlights.

'You see what I mean?' Rick is saying, his head jiving up and down and not looking at the road at all, 'You see?'

***

The morning shift at McDonald's. A slow morning. I'm shaky after last night but okay. When I woke up the bad taste was back and when I got to work LeRoi shouted at me because I was late and said this was pretty much my last chance and I didn't say anything and so now I've been on the register serving breakfasts for a couple of hours when this girl walks in and I'm like fuck, she's beautiful, then I'm like, fuck, it's the girl we saw in the house, I'm sure of it. It's her. The same girl.

Her skin is sort of milky pale as if she stays away from the light and her hair is straight and glossy and wow, she is really, really beautiful. As if to be extra sure, I can see her Mercedes, parked right by the door – the same one we saw outside the house – and she walks up to me and looks me in the eye, or seems to, because her eyes are hidden by huge sunglasses but I can still feel them, her eyes, like beams of light penetrating into me and she says, 'May I use your bathroom?' in a voice that chills me like ice cubes dropped in a glass of lemonade. From her accent I can tell she sure as hell ain't from round here but then I can't tell where she's from either and I don't say nothing so she walks straight past and goes into the ladies'. I'm interrupted by some jerk who expects me to take his order so I press the relevant buttons, take his money and give him his change and then I see the girl walk out again. She doesn't order anything but of course, she wouldn't. She gets back into her car and away she goes.

For some reason I can't really explain I leave the register and ignoring LeRoi I go to the restrooms.

I enter the ladies.

There are two cubicles, both empty. One of the cisterns is hissing as it re-fills with water as if someone has just flushed the toilet so I think that must be the toilet she used and without really being able to say why I go into the cubicle, bend down and sniff, trying to detect her scent, the thing in the air that she has left. It's all I can do not to lick the seat. As I leave the cubicle I notice something gleaming by the sink. A ring, silver and ornate, abandoned in a small puddle. The girl must have taken it off to wash her hands and forgot to put it back on. Quickly, I pocket the object.

On my break I sit out back by the dumpsters, smoking and inspecting the ring. I was hoping the girl might return for it and I could say 'here it is ma'am, I kept it safe for you' and she would be pleased. It's very pretty and fine, with a double raised band that weaves around it. Why did she leave it behind? I can't shake the feeling it all means something. I only saw her a moment, but it's like she's burnt into my mind. We know vampires are meant to be irresistibly attractive. Rick says so but we know it anyway. They give you a hard-on even as they suck the blood out of you. That's why they're so dangerous. I know it's true. Everyone does.

Without really knowing why, I slip the ring onto my finger. It just about fits, but it's tight. Then I can't take it off. It's stuck. Fuck!

We're not allowed to wear jewellery while we're at work in case it contaminates the food or something. I pull hard but it makes no difference. For a minute I panic – I feel hot and scared and violated by this metal thing. I wonder if Rick is right and they are vampires and she left the ring deliberately in the bathroom to trap me. Maybe I'm in their power?... My break only lasts half an hour and somehow I manage to calm down enough to go back to the till. If LeRoi notices anything, he doesn't say so.

***

Rick and me drive out past beyond Bethel towards the abandoned church and the cemetery at Red Hook. It's relentlessly hot and the sky looks like a plastic bag wrapped around a light – bulging, melting, ready to burst into flames. The bad taste in my mouth is overwhelming, as if I breakfasted on ground-up machinery and I still can't get the ring off. The skin around my finger is red and sore from pulling and it feels tight. I tried using soap and water to slide it off, then I tried butter, then oil but nothing worked. I slept with it on and had some sort of trippy dream about a glass house in a great red wasteland. But now I'm here and Rick's saying his dad called and said that Rick should expect him back in the next couple of days. Rick doesn't look at me as he says this and for the first time in ages his mind seems to be on something other than the vampires in the house.

We stop for a minute or two by the old church. My head starts to hurt and I'm feeling nauseous. Rick seems really tense, chewing gum, not saying much. His sunglasses reflect the dull hot sky.

We go outside. The steeple and clapboard walls of the church sag, as if the structure was swamped by a great flood then left to dry out. The sky and trees behind are flat, and it makes me think everything has been strung up for a cheap window display. Long grass curls around our ankles, the air filled with tiny black flies. The heat seems worse and I feel really sick. I can't remember the last time I ate and when I catch sight of myself in the rear-view mirror it's a surprise, my face not so much a real face as a sketch of a face, my eyes like smudgy holes, a few rough lines here and there and a crude scribble for a mouth. A kid could do a better job. It's not much of a face. It's not much of anything.

'I saw them bring the body out here,' Rick points to the cemetery across the road from the church. We walk over. A modern cemetery, the graves stretching away in straight rows and marked with clean, white crosses. A man tends the grass with a strimmer, keeping the edges straight. I'm so high my thoughts are jumping like hot popping bugs and I can't shake the feeling that the rows are shifting one way and another. I try and tell Rick about the vampire girl and how beautiful she was, so hot I could have licked the toilet seat, and she must have left the ring behind, as a sign, a way of warning us because now it's stuck and it hurts. Rick doesn't say anything. His teeth rub together like his face is about to fall to pieces.

***

Ma and her friend Leslie from Walmart are sitting at the table playing cards and smoking and drinking JDs with Diet Coke. The TV is on, Action News covering a hostage situation near Mobile. Some guy stormed Taco Bell with a gun and a grudge. I can tell Ma is real mad at me and she says LeRoi phoned and said something about how I could forget about coming back to work and I think shit I actually cannot remember when my shift was or how I managed to miss it or anything. I think about calling LeRoi back and trying to explain but it's too late and anyway it's easier to stay in my room and get high, like my head, my finger, my cock, my spine, my heart are swelling up so hard I might burst all over the room, so I dance around but trying to be quiet because I'm hyper-aware of Ma and Leslie next door, laughing haw haw haw like they do and I move around, grinding my teeth together until they become fangs, visions of a cold mist pooling through the window and filling the room until the vampire girl is there.

But she isn't. Not really.

***

No, what really happens is this: Rick's dad is back.

We're sitting in Rick's trailer. Rick's dad is in the chair where Rick usually sits. Rick's dad isn't alone. He's brought a friend from prison, a man called Rawlins or Rawson, something like that. I don't quite catch his name. We've been drinking bourbon for hours and have moved on to coke. Rick's dad has a big block of the stuff and he's chopping out lines with a razor blade. It's real dark in the trailer and it's real dark outside and there is a flickering, burnt sort of smell in the air like it's going to thunder but I don't think it will. Rick's dad is smaller than Rick but scarier. Rick's dad has a shaven head with a tattoo on the back of his neck made to look like stitches. It's so hot he's taken off his shirt and his body is skinny but tough, not an inch of flab or slack flesh, just tight muscle and bone and there's a big scar running down from his collarbone to his crotch as if someone cut him open with an axe. More tattoos on his arm, words in Gothic script and on his back a big tattoo of a weeping angel and on one bicep a skull in a ball of fire. Rick's dad is even scarier than I remembered, as if prison has allowed him to carve out a harder version of himself.

Then there's Rick's dad's friend Rawson or Rawlins who is even scarier than Rick's dad. He's huge, six foot six or seven and pumped up like he eats nothing but T-bone steak and steroids. He's also shaved his head but has a tight goatee around his mouth. When he speaks I can see his teeth are all fucked up and dirty, like broken down tombstones and his eyes are really small, as if his face sucked them halfway back inside and his ears are these chewed up little things, his features somehow shrunken against his big, round head. He's wearing a black T-shirt and black jeans and drinks bourbon like it's water and snorts the coke in great fat lines, hoovering it up and sitting back and rubbing his nose. 'Aaargh man,' he says. 'Aaargh fuck yeah,' and then he looks right at me like I'm just a worm he could squash without even thinking about it. I'm on edge for all sorts of reasons. Rick's dad has gone and got out all the guns he left in the trailer for Rick to look after. There's the .357 Magnum, the hunting rifle, a twelve-gauge shotgun, the Browning Hi-Power automatic and the Colt M1911 he once used to fuck up some gangsters down in Albany and, pride of place, the Uzi SMG which Rick once showed me, locked in its box, but never dared to touch. All these guns on the table like we're about to go to war, but then I know Rick's dad is real fond of firearms and I guess having been inside for so long he's missed them, rather like you might miss women or watching whatever you want on TV.

Rick's dad and Rick's dad's friend are talking about the state penitentiary in Alabama and from what they're saying I don't like the sound of prison one bit. I gather Rawlins was incarcerated for even longer than Rick's dad and I wonder what it was he did and that makes me even more frightened. We drink more bourbon and snort more coke and smoke some meth and then Rick starts to tell them about the vampires.

'Ain't never much going on in the day,' he says. 'They keep the curtains closed, everything shut up. Sometimes the old woman and the younger girl go into town. They go to the drugstore. Always dressed in black, eyes hidden with sunglasses, you know. I ain't never seen the man. I ain't never seen them before and they sure ain't from round here. There wasn't nobody lived in that house for years.'

'The house by I-5?' says Rick's dad.

'Yeah.'

'Someone did live there,' he goes on, 'but they was always real solitary, that's as far as I can recall. Anyhow, that was a long time ago.' He rubs his face.

'You see bats?' asks Rawlins. 'Lotsa bats around the house?'

'All the time.' Rick nods.

'I reckon so,' says Rick's dad, nodding sagely like this is all normal.

'The one they buried,' says Rick. 'We ought to dig up the coffin, then we'd know for sure.'

I want to say something but I'm so scared and high and there's this weird black energy floating about the room and the bad taste in my mouth just won't go and I sense we're going forward, real fast and there's nothing I can do. Rick's dad burps and picks his teeth with a toothpick. 'Rawlins,' he says, 'shall we tell the boys 'bout that time?'

'Yeah man,' Rawlins smiles an ugly smile. 'Tell 'em.'

'Don't you never doubt there's no such thing as vampires.' Rick's dad leans forward and looks right at me, like he's read my mind, sensed my doubts. 'Not when you seen what we seen.'

'That's right.' Rawlins nods.

'One time they brought this prisoner in. He was being transferred from somewhere else. That ain't the point. Dude was inside for the rape and murder of a little girl near Mobile. Big, sick nigger, weren't he? The boy was marked, you know?'

'Sure was.'

'We all knew it, the guards knew it, everyone did. They made the sign during dinner one evening. One of the brotherhood went over and spat on the floor in front of him. Well, none of his people were gonna help. Them other niggers stayed well away.'

'It's like that inside.' Rawlins licks his lips with a long, black tongue.

'It happened noon next day. We was all out in the yard. If you think about it, they shouldn't have even allowed that nigger out but they wanted it to happen. Someone arranged something with the warden. Everyone knew. These things is all organised from on high.' He stabs his index finger at the table. 'Strike of noon and suddenly all the guards just walked away, you remember that Rawlins?'

'Couldn't forget.'

'Two of the brotherhood knocked him down. One of them had a razor, pulled off the sick nigger's trousers and cuts his balls off just as sure as if he was cutting the throat of a hog. The man held up his balls like a trophy. Meanwhile, the nigger is screamin' and bleedin' everywhere but that was just the start. See,' he leans forward, grinning, and all I can see are his yellow teeth, 'they'd let out this prisoner they normally keep in solitary. He was on death row, dude by the name of Lawhorn, Victor Lawhorn. He was a legend in the penitentiary because of how long he'd been there although almost no one had ever seen him. They said he was a cannibal.'

'They said he was a vampire.'

'That's right.' Rick's dad nods. 'So they brings him out, all pale like a skeleton 'cause they keep him away from the light, you know? Everyone watching, our people on one side, niggers and Mexicans on the other, nigger writhing on the ground and Lawhorn walked forward and bent down and tore out the man's throat with his own teeth. He more or less ripped that fucking nigger's head off. Then he took off his shirt and rubbed himself in the fresh blood. Now, I've seen some bad shit, but in all my days I ain't never seen shit like that before.' He bends forward, snorting another line of coke. He rubs his teeth and coughs. 'When it was all done he walked back to his cell, calm and cool as anything. The guards came back to clean up the mess and that was all. We don't know what they do with the body. Lawhorn went back into solitary, back to death row, but he ain't never gonna die, understand?'

'Some of them,' says Rawlins, 'they claim Lawhorn been on death row since 1940. He been inside a real long time but then when you can live forever it's all relative, ain't it? All he need was a little human blood now and then. Governor and such too 'fraid to send him to the chair 'cause they know he can escape jus' soon as he wants to. These sorts of things, there ain't much a man like us can do about it, except be disgusted at all the filth, all the scum, all the dirt they have in there. The things they put us through.' He lights a cigarette, his face twisted with disgust. 'These fucking niggers. Usurping the white man's power. Taking our place. Overturning the order.'

'You wouldn't believe what we seen.' Rick's dad rubs one hand over his jaw.

'Covey, Covey man, tell them about the ring,' says Rick.

'I got this ring,' I say, holding out my finger.

'Let me see that.' Rawlins seizes me. His hand is huge and he twists me round. 'Shit, that's a fine piece of jewellery. Look at that.' Rick's dad bends over. He takes my finger and pulls at the ring. His fingers are hard like metal wire. An excruciating pain runs up my hand and I cry out but the ring pops off. Rick's dad holds it up. 'Mighty fine.' He nods in agreement. 'Where did you get this?'

'The girl from the house – she left it behind where Covey works,' Rick interrupts.

'You got this from the girl in the house?'

I nod. My finger really hurts.

Rick's dad and Rawlins exchange a look. 'Rick,' says Rick's dad.

'Yes Pa.'

Rick's dad picks up his Uzi. He holds it lovingly, turning it this way and that, a strange smile on his lips.

'Come boys. What say we go vampire huntin'?'

'Yeah?' Rick almost leaps out of his chair, like he doesn't know what to do or where to go.

Rick's dad and Rawlins start laughing, their heads thrown back, their mouths open so wide it's like they might try to eat their own face. 'You're a good boy,' Rick's dad paws the back of his head. 'You're stupid, but you're a good boy.'

Rawlins jerks round to look straight at me. He's still laughing. It's all I can do not to piss myself.

HOPE'S END

I received news from my esteemed colleague, Professor William Dyer, concerning an archaeological discovery in North Dakota of considerable importance and – as I am an expert on Neolithic American cultures – I decided to assist in the excavations. It was the summer and with my teaching duties finished for the next few months I thought it might be amenable to drive from Cornell to the site with my lover, Jessica Bray. As an Englishman and an expatriate, I was curious to see more of the United States than afforded by the pleasant confines of my campus town. Stimulated by the prospect of a road trip, I hoped the change of scene might help to revive my relationship with Jessica, which, due to the pressures of my research and her own anxieties concerning the completion of her thesis on Mayan harvest rituals, had entered what we might call rather choppy waters.

We were five days in. I purposefully sought to avoid major cities and took us on a somewhat circumspect route, cutting through upstate Pennsylvania and into Ohio, traversing the lakes before turning south through Indiana, Illinois and into Iowa. From Iowa, the plan was to take Highway 29 into the Dakotas and to the site, some thirty miles or so from the fracking boom town of Stanley. So far I'd been somewhat dismayed by what I'd seen on our travels, the American sublime soiled by sloughs of deplorable suburban sprawl, dismal drive-thrus, vulgar Walmarts and ghastly retail parks built with the apparent intention of offending all aesthetic sense. Determined to find a more authentic, rustic America, I opted for ever more obtuse routes, ill-trodden back roads through nameless little hamlets and slumbering burgs. Jessica had grown increasingly sullen, complaining of car sickness and, being a vegetarian, bemoaning the poor quality food found in highway dining areas. She is a rather contrary young lady, a native Californian with an encyclopaedic knowledge of eating disorders and food allergies. Alas, our little jaunt was beginning to have an effect antithetical to my original hopes and I found myself beginning to question our entire liaison. I am, after all, more than thirty years her senior with a vengeful ex-wife somewhere back in England and enough hang-ups and neuroses of my own to keep the campus psychotherapist amply entertained. Although charmed by Jessica's youth, the tedium of having to manage her chronically low self-esteem was beginning to wear me down. I was also beginning to wonder what she actually saw in me. I used to be quite the silver fox, as they say, but I have to admit I'm past my prime. No, I'm beginning to suspect – as is common with such liaisons – that the moment she passes her viva our relationship, such as it is, will be well and truly over

Anyway, I digress. At present, we are somewhere in west Iowa, driving through a flat terrain of fields neatly divided by perfectly straight roads. The weather has turned very hot and Jessica is paying no attention whatsoever to my exposition on the significance of the grid in the spatial configuration of the American mindset. The point, as I'm trying to explain, is that the grid eliminates mystery, it removes the possibility of a wrong turn and so, whereas Europe is configured by the mazy twists and turns of a complex history, the remorseless organisation of the American Midwest represents the conquest of reason over space and, in turn, the domination of space over time.

'You're only saying that because we're lost,' Jessica chides, rolling her brown eyes at me with the disdain young people reserve for the foibles of the old.

We pass through a melancholy settlement, a forlorn outpost of abandoned silos and warehouses, the gaunt structures stranded in an overgrown field. Off the main road, I glimpse a few small houses – little more than shacks or trailers – squat under lush trees. Aside from a single tattered Stars and Stripes and a couple of pick-up trucks pulled up outside one of the dwellings, the whole place appears almost entirely abandoned. I'm rather charmed by the sight, the nearest one could hope to find – so I muse to Jessica – to a ruined castle or Roman settlement although she doesn't seem particularly taken by the comparison. Of course, there is still the question of the discoveries in Dakota and I'm thrilled by the pictures sent to me by Professor Dyer of a great hole descending deep into the earth, but in lieu of such a marvel I conclude that we have to make do with the more mundane remnants of the industrial age.

'We're not lost,' I chide, reaching over to pat her leg. Much to my surprise, Jessica grabs my wrist and presses my hand against her thigh. Due to the hot weather she is wearing a short skirt and no tights. As she does this, Jessica looks at me with a most peculiar intensity and, holding fast to my wrist, moves my hand upwards into the nebulous, fuzzy warmth of her crotch.

'What are you doing?' I exclaim. 'I'm driving for heaven's sake!'

'What do you think I'm doing,' she counters.

'Well...'

'Oh you're so boring! Just pull over goddamit and fuck me.'

'Jessica!' I must admit, I'm shocked. This is most unlike her. Jessica tends to be rather prudish and when it comes to putting my 'thingy' in her 'fu-fu' as she calls it, we prefer not to talk while doing it or indeed to talk about it at all, opting for coitus in the bedroom, lying down with the lights out. Nonetheless, an 'atmosphere', as one might say, had, as it were, 'emerged' between us and perhaps this was the reason for all her moans and myriad petty frustrations.

'Fuck me you old fart!' she snarls again pulling my hand harder so that my fingers slip under her knickers. Good Lord. She is, as I imagine freshmen and jocks might say, very wet. The car lurches across the middle of the road. I brake hard and pull up by the verge.

'What if someone comes,' I protest.

'Who cares?' She hikes up her skirt and clambers on top of me. 'We haven't seen another car for ages anyway.'

Before I recount the following, I should say that all this is most unlike me. Naturally, in my time I've had a modest share of rumpy-pumpy although my ex-wife said I was a 'boring' lover and in recent years there have been many occasions when the old 'thingy' has just not been up to the job. Still, I like to think there's a bit of gas – as our American cousins call it – left in the tank, that I still have a few old tricks to teach the young. In any case, Jessica and I are at it like a couple of lusty Romans and before I know it I am overwhelmed with the mightiest orgasm while she tells me to 'fill her with cum' (words I have never before heard her utter) – a request with which I duly comply.

I disengage, out of breath, a cramp in my thigh and my heart going like the clappers. Jessica pulls away, straightens her skirt and gives me a look of languid contentment at odds with her habitual demeanour of bitter dissatisfaction.

Our relief does not last long. Glancing in the rear-view mirror, I see a patrol car parked up a few feet behind us and a sheriff strolling forward, his wide-brimmed hat pulled low over his face.

'Sweet Jesus,' I cry, 'it's the police!' frantically zippering myself back up.

Nonchalant, the sheriff raps on the window.

''Scuse me,' he says.

I quickly wind it down. 'Afternoon officer, how are you? We were, um, we were just discussing the route. I was checking the map.' I'm babbling.

The sheriff squints at me. The map is in the back. He looks at Jessica. 'Miss, are you all right? Has this man been bothering you?'

'No, no, I'm fine. Not at all,' Jessica garbles.

The sheriff takes a moment. 'I was watching back there and it looked like... well, I just wanted to make sure.'

'We're all fine, thanks, don't worry, will that be all?'

'Is this your car, sir?'

'My car? No, I mean yes, I mean no, it's a hire car, it belongs to Hertz.'

'May I see your license?'

'Is there a problem officer? There's no problem is there? Officer?'

'License, please.'

I fumble around in my wallet, find my license and pass it over. The sheriff takes it and wanders back to his patrol car. I can see him say something into his radio.

'Bloody hell!' I snap at Jessica. 'I just knew this was going to happen. It's all your fault. What are we going to do now?'

'Oh stop worrying.'

'Stop worrying! Stop worrying! I've got my career to think about. I've got tenure! I've got—'

'Just cut it out!'

The sheriff returns. 'I'm sorry sir,' he leans over and leers at us. 'I'm going to have to ask you to follow me back to the station.'

'The station! What! What are you talking about?' I gaze at the sheriff in astonishment, hoping for a trace of compassion in his leathery face, for something, anything I might be able to appeal to. But alas, I see nothing. 'Officer,' I protest, 'my name is Professor—'

'I know your name *sir*, it was on your license.'

'No, you don't understand, I have to get to North Dakota...'

'North Dakota? What are you doing here then?'

'The point is – oh look – there is an archaeological discovery of unprecedented importance. An excavation. They need my expertise. I'm an expert, you see...'

'Sir, I'm going to ask you to follow me back to the station. It's only a few miles back that way.' The sheriff briefly touches his hand to his hat in a half-hearted salute and walks back to his car.

'Jesus! What are we going to do now?'

'Well, we have to do what he says.'

'Of course we have to do what he says. Oh bloody hell. I hope you're happy now.'

'Don't blame me. It's not my fault!'

'Wench!'

'Don't call me that, dirty old man!'

'Oh just listen to us!' I bang the wheel with frustration.

Well, I won't repeat the rest of our predictable and tawdry argument. As the accusations bounce back and forth we follow the sheriff to the deserted looking township we'd passed through earlier and pull up outside a modest single-storey building, the same one I noticed before, flying a solitary Stars and Stripes. As we get out, I take a moment to survey the scene. There really is nothing, just a few run-down buildings scattered seemingly at random around the road, old shops or whatnot, shut-up and abandoned. The sun is remorselessly hot, the air very still. I smell a dried out, desiccated sort of smell, insect-like, close and uncomfortable and I realise we are being watched from across the road – a couple of figures in a doorway, their silhouettes sun-stretched across the hot tarmac. Beyond the shacks, flat fields of corn to the horizon. Christ. The sheriff puts one callused hand on my arm and ushers me into the station.

'Hey Hank,' he calls out to another officer – his deputy I assume – who is sat with his feet on the desk.

'Howdy Carl.'

'Got us another two,' says the sheriff.

'So I see.'

'C'mon in folks. This here's a British professor.'

'A professor?'

'That's right.'

'Well I'll be.'

'Take a seat.' He gestures at Jessica, who sits down on a plastic chair. I stand there while these two bumpkin enforcers gawp at me as if they have never seen a British professor before. Trying to hold myself aloof, I take a moment to assess my surroundings. The office is a dismal little space with a dirty parquet floor, grubby pot plants wilting in the heat and dead flies stuck to yellowed glass. There are two desks piled high with papers and the wall behind the deputy is covered in faded wanted posters, an assemblage of rather desperate looking African-Americans and mean-faced rednecks.

'Well now.' The sheriff takes off his hat and wipes his forehead. He's quite an old man, almost as old as me, his neck and forehead creased and worn as if he's been folded up many times over. He exudes a thick-necked masculine quality, a strong odour of tobacco and musty aftershave. I imagine he likes to drink Bud, watch the game and rail against the federal government, one of those God-fearing gun-loving abortion-hating Republican-voting American men I've always found rather repulsive and, from an intellectual point of view, quite incomprehensible. His deputy is a little younger, but not much, a lanky, squinty-eyed fellow with a narrow hatchet face and a long-hooked nose that makes him resemble a grumpy witch hunter from the time of Cotton Mather.

This state of affairs cannot continue. I must take charge. 'Officer.' I draw myself up and prep my voice. A superior English accent can do wonders over here, I find, triggering some sort of subconscious Pavlovian colonial instinct for deference particularly among our more provincial and insular transatlantic cousins. 'Officer, I am the Randolph C. Carter Professor of Ancient American Cultures at Cornell University. My scholarship on primitive North American society is foremost in the field. I'm on the board of numerous academic presses and editor-in-chief of *Neolithicus*. I'm a recipient of two Leverhulmes, a Guggenheim fellowship and—'

The sheriff cuts me off with a raised hand. 'I'm arresting you, professor, for an act of gross public indecency.'

I feel as if I've been slapped in the face. 'Why – how dare you! Absurd. Preposterous. Good god. How dare you!' Flabbergasted, I feel my face burn.

The sheriff yawns, 'Our vehicles are equipped with cameras. I can show you the proof, if you want to see it again.'

I won't stand for this. 'Outrageous. I demand to call my lawyer.' I turn to glare at Jessica. The stupid girl just sits there, dumbfounded, gobsmacked. Didn't she tell me her father is some sort of hot-shot L.A. attorney? I reach for my mobile. 'I won't stand for this.' I wasn't sure who to call. The police? The FBI? Can I claim wrongful arrest? I don't actually have a lawyer. What to do? Anyway, it's all in vain. No signal. Jessica was complaining earlier about the lack of reception. The sheriff and his deputy continue to look at me with thinly veiled amusement. I put my phone away.

'Nearest lawyer is all the way in Midtown,' says the sheriff, 'and he won't be able to get over here until tomorrow morning.'

'It's true,' his deputy nods.

Well, I tell you now, I wasn't going to put up with this any longer. 'Indecent behaviour... How dare you! I don't want some two-bit lawyer. Outrageous. How dare you! Who the hell do you think you are?'

'It's the law, sir—'

My blood is boiling. 'The law? The law? Who the hell are you to tell me about the law?' It's hard to describe what happened next. My voice rose in pitch and tone and I think I said 'bloody hell' quite a number of times. I remember instructing Jessica to go back to the car and told her and the sheriff that we were leaving. Apparently this wasn't allowed because the next thing I knew the sheriff and his deputy had manhandled me into a small room. They slammed the door in my face and turned the key. Great Scott! One minute I'd been driving peaceably through the American countryside, preoccupied with whether Professor Dyer's discoveries would support or invalidate my famous Delaware Hypothesis concerning tool use among Neolithic Amerindians and now I'm in a cell. A police cell for criminals! I continue to bang on the door, shouting about my rights and other such things. Indeed, I believe I may have recited a large part of Jefferson's declaration, not to mention a good chunk of Rousseau and possibly even some Voltaire for good measure, not that these cretinous enforcement agents take any notice. Eventually, I calm down. Whilst true that Jessica and had been caught *in flagrante* I'm fairly sure the sheriff's methods were cack-handed and once I get a good lawyer on the case I'd be released with an apology to boot. No, my real concern was the damage to my reputation if news of this got out. The last thing I wanted was scandal. There had, after all, been one or two other incidents. That silly undergraduate girl many years back that led, eventually, to the collapse of my marriage, and since then, well... perhaps best not to dwell on such indiscretions. I have been a slave to my research, but I have not always been, it must be said, a perfect man. No, I prefer to think of my life as a checkerboard, the black marks enlivened by enough spots of brilliance to muster some respect, some acknowledgement that I, Graham Coxworth-Grove have made a contribution, however small, to our civilisation and that the great wall of human understanding, the bridge and battlements of knowledge have been fortified by my work. I hope that, thanks to my endeavours, the barbarians may be kept from the gates just a little longer. Generations of young people, instructed in my methods and shown the gifts of my superior reasoning, will go forth to continue my work. My research will endure, I know this much, as a beacon to aid those that dare to ascend after me into the foothills and mountaintops of learning.

I'm still shouting and banging when the door of the cell is flung open – lo – the sheriff and his lanky deputy. I'm about to demand my release when the sheriff raises his arm and sprays something in my face. My eyes burn, my nose fills with an excruciating substance. I cannot breathe,

I cannot see! My hands go up, my knees go down. A sharp jolt in my arm, a burning smell and then the void...

...Strung out in the cold darkness... I am a press-ganged lookout clutching at the rigging of a ship adrift in Arctic seas... I am an astronomer locked in the dungeons of the Inquisition... I am a psychoanalyst fleeing Austria across icy Alpine footpaths... I don't know where I am... who I am... As is my habit during periods of stress, I soothe myself by reciting the genus homo, my mind skipping over that long line of evolution that stretches from tender-footed *homo habilis* and *homo rudolfensis* stumbling upright through the primeval forest to *homo georgicus, homo nonsensicus, homo ergaster* and *homo erectus* – human prototypes banging bones together and staring into the flickering campfire. And how can I forget rare *homo cepranensis* or *homo antecessor, homo heidelbergensis* and *homo rhodesiensis*... think of them, waging war on the Neanderthals in the steppes of Gondwanaland... man at the dawn of the human epoch... the ragged edge of possibility...

And then, alas, my present discomfort was too much to endure. Floating back to consciousness, I open my eyes.

Words, at this moment, fail me.

I dislike admitting it. I am not, after all, an inarticulate man. I am the author of four books, not to mention nearly three dozen articles and countless papers and presentations. My second book, *Acheulean Tool Use in the Lower Paleolithic* won two major awards and has since been recognised as the definitive text on the subject. I have supervised twenty-three PhDs and examined around a hundred. I have taught thousands of hours of classes, seminars, supervisions. I have marked tens of thousands of undergraduate essays.

As a diversion from my research, I have also written two collections of poetry, published at my own expense. For the first, *Ruminations on the Fall of Darjeeling*, I assumed the persona of a melancholy colonialist lamenting the decline of the British Empire and for the second, *Big Boom*, I became Canetti Cannelloni, a far-right Futurist from Bologna. The central conceit of this volume, which most amused me, was the introduction of a second persona, a certain Dr Palimpscheisser, who was purported to have translated the volume from the original Italian on the basis of a single surviving manuscript kept now in the private museum of a Milanese collector.

Unfortunately, none of this was going to be of any use.

I appear to be tied to a stake in the middle of a cornfield. I've been lashed up quite thoroughly and am stuck fast. It is dark and surprisingly cold. Indeed, the inclement air is more suggestive of a damp cellar or tomb than the open spaces of the Midwest. On the horizon, a faint blue light flickers like a distant TV set or neon sign, but I cannot identify the source of the illumination. No moon graces the heavens and the few stars seem very faint and far. I see several more stakes stuck at intervals in the field. One or two appear to have things hanging from them, tatty rags like bits of scarecrows. Much of the corn has been broken down and I can just discern a motley assemblage of objects scattered hither and thither – a deflated tyre, dismantled portions of agricultural machinery, burnt tangles of clothing.

There is something else. I am not alone.

'Well professor, here we are.' The sheriff and his deputy stand below me.

'What's going on? Why are you doing this?' My voice is rather weak. My mouth bitterly dry, my tongue stuck like a desiccated sausage in my pensive jaw.

'This here be a region cursed by God.'

'Cursed by God? My dear fellow, don't be so ridiculous.' I know I must keep reasoning with them. It's the only way. 'Its economics, I mean, without subsidies, it's very hard, isn't it? To compete, you know, as a farmer. I daresay people have gone to the city...'

'The purgin' wiped out enough of 'em,' says the deputy.

'I beg your pardon.'

'There be a war across these plains.'

'War? Between whom?'

'Between them that are saved and those that choose the other way.'

I gaze at the two men. They must be joking.

The deputy steps forward. 'Now, as you probably guessed, somethin' bad is goin' to happen.'

'Right. I mean, no. I don't follow.'

'Well, you be tied to a stake in a field in the dead of night. It don't look so good, does it now?'

This much is true. 'So, what are you going to do?'

'We ain't goin' to do nothin'.'

'You's an offering. A sacrifice,' says the sheriff. 'As we said, this here be a region cursed by God.'

We clearly aren't getting anywhere. I find my voice again. 'Chaps, look here, I'm afraid I still don't quite follow. I do rather need the toilet and these ropes are hurting my arms. Can't we be reasonable?'

'This be a haunted region, one watched over by He Who Must Be Pleased.'

'Oh, do spare me this nonsense.'

'Could be the restless souls of dead Indians or pioneers who was killed by Indians when they first came to the region or else it could be settlers what froze to death in the winter or else the ghosts of outlaws and bandits killed in fights with the law or else the vengeful spirits of abandoned orphans or maybe it's got something to do with runaway slaves or an ancient evil what's been buried here since before the time of man. We don't know.'

'We don't really care,' the deputy adds. 'We do what we have to.'

'And what's that?'

'Leave you here 'til mornin'.'

'What about Jessica?'

'My wife is lookin' after her.'

'But...'

'Her fate depends on yours. Hopefully, come morning, it will all be clear. Have a good night now.' The sheriff doffs his Stetson and the two men turn away and disappear into the dark corn.

I hang on a while, waiting, my bladder fit to burst and my thoughts, by this stage, rather discombobulated. I'm sure I can hear something, shuffling and sliding like a great serpent through the corn. It must be the sheriff and his deputy, come back to cut me down having satisfied whatever malicious spirit had led them to treat me with such cruelty. My word, when I get out of here, there's going to be hell to pay!

***

From: Dyer, W (William.Dyer@cornell.edu)
To: Coxworth-Grove, G (g.coxworthgrove@cornell.edu)
Coxer!
Where are you? You were supposed to get here two days ago. What's going on? Do you never answer your phone? Did you get the e-mail I sent? We need you here. I've made a rather troubling discovery. I haven't even begun to absorb what it could mean but we might have to rethink our assumptions. Anyway, I'm worried. There have been numerous unforeseen problems. The graduate students I brought along to help have all fallen ill and we don't know what's wrong. Some sort of skin irritation coupled with distressing hallucinations. And that's not all. I knew I should have never hired those Mexicans. They refuse to work anymore even though I've offered to double their wages. They seem to think we've violated a sacred place. There is more, but I'll have to tell you face to face. You won't believe it until you see what I've found. Hurry!
  William

ACTION TV NEWS!
NEWSFLASH!
This is live!

We are going to an interview with Jessica Bray, the Cornell student who, as viewers will be aware, went missing with her professor, Graham Coxworth-Grove in Iowa three days ago. Let's go live to Midtown, Iowa.

Jessica!

Jessica, tell us what happened?

– Oh my God it was horrible. I've had, like, a totally awful time. Professor Coxworth told me he needed me to come with him to some archaeological site and he said I could assist in the excavations and everything. He said it would help with my dissertation.

What happened, Jessica?

What did he do to you?

– Lies! He lied to me. We never even got to the site. We just drove for days through state after state. He wouldn't tell me where we were going or why. And, it's totally gross but he made me do things to him at night, in the motels and sometimes in the car... It was horrible (sob)...

He didn't!

No!

That's disgusting!

What did you do?

– The first chance I had I just like totally ran away. I like just totally ran. He came after me so I ran deeper and deeper into the fields. He kept calling me but I wouldn't go back. Eventually I got away from him, but I was lost. I mean Iowa right? It's like totally empty. I spent the night out there. Eventually this nice sheriff found me and brought me to safety. I just want to thank Sheriff Carl Connor and all the good people of Hope's End, Iowa. Oh my gosh they are just about the nicest people I've ever met anywhere. Thank you all so much for your support and help.

Sheriff!

Sheriff Carl Connor!

Tell us your story sheriff!

– Well folks, when we found Jessica she was in a state of shock. From what we can tell, she was lucky to get away from this pervert. Hope's End is a nice small town full of good clean people who mind their own business and we all want to make sure it stays that way.

What about the pervert professor?

What you going to do about him?

– We've circulated his details to the FBI and all the relevant authorities. The net is closing. He won't get far.

ACTION TV NEWS!

Police have given us this new photofit of the pervert professor. Check it out! Anyone with information about his whereabouts should phone the number below. And now, with reports of a mystery illness in a remote part of North Dakota, we cut to our reporter Jed Blankman. Jed, what's the story out there?

EXPLODING ZOMBIE COCK

So, anyway, it was at this moment Rich reached into his rucksack to produce a small, amber coloured vial. 'Here,' he said, 'this is what I'm talking about.'

'Bro,' said Brock.

Rich put the vial on the table. It was like a child's medicine bottle, Calpol, something like that, dark coloured glass wrapped in a plastic bag. Rich sniffed and wiped his beard with a bangle-adorned wrist. 'Be careful with this guys, it contains a whole host of weird shit, things like datura stramonium, velvet bean, bearded fireworm, angel trumpet, cane toad, puffer fish, tarantula, red python and, finally,' he swallowed and touched his mouth, 'the ground bones of a human child.'

'No shit.' Brock was impressed.

'Are you serious?' I asked.

'Bro,' Rich turned his attention to me for the first time. 'What do you think I've been doing in Haiti for the last four months?' Brock told me earlier that Rich works for the UN and likes to stop by when he's in NYC with something special from whichever trouble spot he has been posted to. 'I've been in motherfucking Port-au-Prince and all sorts of places you wouldn't believe trying to help pull that shithole back together. Yes, dude, this is for real. I got this from a bokor of the highest order, a man well-schooled in the old ways.'

'What's a bokor?' asked Brock.

'A witchdoctor dude. A shaman.'

'How do you know it works?' I added.

'I don't, not for sure. Sometimes the ingredients are active. Sometimes not. But man,' he removed his glasses and looked at Brock and me with red-rimmed eyes. 'I saw some crazy things out there. If you want to make a zombie this is what you need.' He slapped his hand on the table.

Brock put the vial in the kitchen cupboard and we all kicked back with a few beers and smokes. Rich regaled us with some good stories about Haiti – the gangsters and child prostitutes, the corruption, the refugee camps after the earthquake, squatters in the remains of the presidential palace conducting desperate voodoo ceremonies where he said he saw a man eat a burning log and another where they slaughtered goats and rubbed the blood over themselves, shit like that.

We all went down to our local. Most of the crew tagged along – Joel and Tao, all those guys, Mookie too. I wanted to ask Mookie what was going on between us but she was evasive and vapid, her eyes as sweet and glazed as an iced bun. 'I can't talk about this right now,' she said. 'It's the Paxil the shrink put me on.' In the end she let me go back to hers where we made out for a bit. She gave me a handjob then sent me home.

In the morning Rich was gone but the vial with the potion was still here.

'What are we going to do with that?' I asked Brock. 'Should we throw it out?'

'Are you crazy? I paid Rich two thousand bucks for it.'

'You're shitting me.'

'Bro, you never know when it might come in useful. There are a lot of people I'd like to turn into a zombie.'

***

Then I guess we just forgot about it for a few weeks. Things went on as if everything was normal. I continued with my semester at Colombia although I wasn't getting quite as much from my course as I'd hoped for when I signed up for the study abroad programme. Sometimes I wonder if I only got in because my scumbag of a father is a professor at Cornell and 'had a word' with someone. I don't know – he studies early human cultures or something, I'm doing political science so perhaps his influence wasn't all that. Anyway... Brock is big in the Brooklyn scene, and his mom kind of knows my dad from back in the day which is how I linked up with him. Brock knows a lot of people and his aunt's brownstone – where we lived rent free on the top floor apartment – is on like the second or third coolest street in the whole of Williamsburg, so it was easy to get distracted. Things got a bit more intense with Mookie and then they went a bit wrong. Apparently, I told her that I'd broken up with Sarah, my girlfriend back in London, but she said she saw a text I sent Sarah telling her I loved her and missed her and Mookie said that sucked and stopped speaking to me which was confusing as I thought she wanted to keep it 'casual' like she said.

Summer came fast on the heels of winter and the weather got very hot, very early. I was feeling bad about things but just sort of drifting. It seemed difficult to change, difficult to make a decision. Sometimes I missed Sarah, sometimes days could go by and I wouldn't think about her at all. She was going to visit but then I was vague and nothing ever happened. The flights got too expensive, whatever. I don't think Brock and the rest would have liked her anyway. In my mind I conceived of all sorts of scenes. Sometimes she'd try and link me on G-chat and I'd quickly go offline and sometimes I'd call her and she wouldn't answer and I'd lie in bed, sweating in the heat, wondering who she was with and what she was doing.

The thing is it's not like I even liked Mookie that much to start with. She's very different to Sarah, with short, messy hair and these big goofy glasses and she wears these funny, shapeless dresses – you couldn't even call them vintage – that made it impossible to tell if she had a hot body or not but then one night she turned what Brock called her 'full beam' onto me and I was like, 'shit, you're really attractive.' It's like Brock told me, 'watch out for her full beam dude,' and then it started, sort of, whatever it was. And she did have quite a good body, I just hadn't seen it right.

The other thing: at first I thought it would be a cinch, being in New York, but that was before I actually came here. Naively, I'd thought Americans were basically the same as English people, if a bit more Christian and open about their feelings and fond of guns, but I was wrong. They're nothing like us, nothing like us at all. They loved my accent, of course. 'Oh my gawd, I just love your accent,' the chicks would say, but that only took me so far. It got me to the first stage, but I don't know if I could ever get to the second. It was the sort of thing I ought to talk about with my father – he's been here for years, ever since he left Mum for some student – but I don't like to talk to him.

They were very tiring, New Yorkers, that's the other thing. Maybe they're not like other Americans, I don't really know. Londoners aren't much like other English people, I guess. It was very hard to know if anyone was my friend or if they were just pretending. Everyone was always trying to get one over everyone else. Everyone was trying to 'make the scene'. I didn't get it. Was Mookie truly upset about Sarah or just acting like it? Did she really want me or was it just a ruse to provoke Tao and some of the other guys? They were all much more successful than me and their parents were much, much richer than mine as well. I knew that much.

During this introspective period Brock said his cousin Ben was coming to stay for a few days. Ben, said Brock, was different. He was from the Kentucky side of the family, not the New York side. He wasn't a literature major. He was in the marines, officer training, a lieutenant, due to be shipped out for his first tour of Afghanistan. 'He's a bit, you know,' said Brock, doing a 'loco' sign with his fingers, 'but looking for a good time before some Taliban blows his balls off. It's our duty to send him off in style.'

The idea didn't come to me until later.

Now, Brock is a dweeby guy whose coolness is in marked disproportion to his size, his tufty goatee and the round bifocals he persists in wearing that magnify his intense brown eyes. He likes skinny jeans that show just how puny his legs are and he's already going bald, despite having just turned twenty-five. He carries around this little Moleskine notebook where he tries to write poems 'in the style of John Ashbery' although all the ones I've read are crap. It doesn't matter though, like I said he's super hooked up, his dad practically founded *Wallpaper* and his mum – as well as knowing my dad from God knows when – dates Jay McInerney or is having an affair with him, something like that. Anyhow he gets to write feature pieces for *N+1* magazine and knows people like Gessen, Heti and Lorentzen, you get the picture. Not that these names meant anything to me until I came here, but I know different now.

Ben was nothing like Brock. When he pitched up at the apartment I thought he was a different species from his cousin, like one of those professional six-pack guys that stand around outside Hollister, handsome, tanned, tall, blond, blue-eyed, square-jawed and white-toothed, his ripped physique clearly visible under his T-shirt. More annoying still, he came across as a decent enough sort of bloke.

I tried to niggle him about Afghanistan in the hope that he might conform to type and start going on about killing rag-heads and that but instead I got all this crap about how pleased he was to be joining what he called 'the brotherhood of the marines', 'serving his country' and 'helping people' and fuck me if he wasn't sincere. He was staying for a week, 'I just want to drink lots of beer and get laid as much as I can.'

'No problem bro,' said Brock.

So, anyway, Joel and Tao came over with Nettie, Colette and Mookie. It was a bit of a surprise to see Mookie as we hadn't really spoken since the Sarah thing. We were kind of drunk and high when they came over. Everyone was bitching about the heat. With her black dress and white bow Mookie looked like an actress from *The Discreet Charm of the Bourgeoisie*. She sort of half nodded at me but then sat at the opposite end of the room, nearest Ben. For some reason, everyone – even Tao – wanted to speak to him. They seemed to think he was some kind of beautiful freak, as if joining the marines – rather than, I don't know, making movies and putting them on YouTube like Tao does, which somehow get like a million hits – was the weirdest thing in the world. Even Joel – who has an even bigger trust fund than Brock and was writing a parody of Joyce called 'Whir' that no-one had read or would ever want to read – was into it.

Ben talked about boot camp and running twenty miles with a fifty-pound backpack and how hard it was to calibrate the angle on a 40mm M203 grenade launcher on a customised M16 rifle and then he told us what it was like to hunt in the Kentucky backwoods and the best way to skin a wild boar. He said the military had built a mock Afghan village in the mountains of Utah, inhabited by real Afghanis. They used the village to practise what was going to happen in Afghanistan – dealing with IEDs, raiding suspect Taliban – all that shit. Apparently some of the real Afghanis had actually been raided by marines, back home in Kandahar or wherever and now they were here, endlessly rehearsing what had happened to them for real.

I drank several beers and rolled a big spliff and smoked most of it. Brock saw that a hashtag about a friend they all knew was trending on Twitter, finally diverting attention from Ben to everyone's phone. The friend was some sort of feminist or maybe an anti-feminist – she was a woman, anyhow and Naomi Wolf had just taken her apart on a current affairs show. Everyone was focused on their screens. I'd never met or even heard of this feminist or anti-feminist and neither had Ben and for a moment we exchanged a glance, something that seemed to say, 'Hey, we're both outsiders here, but it's cool, we understand one another' and I thought maybe, just maybe this guy is okay.

Then Mookie touched his arm.

The moment was broken. He leant close to respond to her. I was quite high and as I watched them all sorts of bad thoughts whizzed through my mind. I tried to think through an outcome that wouldn't end with Ben sleeping with Mookie. At the same time, because I don't want to be morbid and anyway, it's not like she's my girlfriend, I don't *love* her, she is a free person and I'm a free person so why should I care anyway? With that in mind I tried to talk to Colette. She was single and I think she slept with Brock – she'd definitely slept with Tao and if she slept with them... but it didn't work, I ended up going on about my assignment. Colette works in a gallery in Tribeca which is fine, but I could tell she wasn't very interested and anyway, my mind wasn't on the conversation, I was just trying to distract myself from whether Mookie was giving Ben 'the full beam' or not.

Wait, I told myself, it was a Sunday, everyone was tired. Nothing ever happens on a Sunday, right?

Wrong.

After some hours there was talk of going to this new club in the Bowery. I said something about how we all had a busy week ahead, but no one was listening. 'Get us some more beers Coxer,' Brock said to me, 'I'll call the car service.' I wish they wouldn't call me Coxer. It's not my fault I have a ridiculous double-barrelled surname. My bloody parents.

Anyway... it's weird, what happened next. I'd like to say I don't know what came over me, but I'm not sure if that's true. It's a bit like this time... well, it's complicated, but it's like a few months ago, just before I came to New York. I persuaded Sarah to let me take some photos of her – on the bed wearing this Ann Summers lingerie I bought her for Valentine's Day. I remember she kept laughing. It didn't come naturally. 'It's not like I'm going to show them to anyone, am I?' I said to her. I offered to let her take some of me but it just seemed to make her even more embarrassed. In the end, I had a spread of about a dozen photos. The funny thing is I then sent them to myexgirlfriend.com where they were put up on the site. It's mild, compared to most of the stuff on there, but sometimes I like to take a look. I get off on her seeing her like that, almost naked and spread out. I wonder how many other guys jerk off to those pictures? I never told her, of course. I don't really understand why I did it, unless it's a sign that I'm what Sarah calls 'a bad person' (she thinks I'm 'a good person' for the record). Who knows? Perhaps I am? My dad is definitely 'a bad person' so perhaps it's inherited?

And perhaps that's also why I sprinkled a little of the zombie powder into Ben's JD and Coke.

Or perhaps it was because, when I went to the kitchen and got a fresh six-pack of beer from the fridge I heard Ben call out: 'Hey, er, Limey dude get me a JD and Coke while you're in there, will you?' Everyone laughed. Everyone.

That was rude.

He was chatting up Mookie and calling me a 'Limey dude'.

So I poured him a large dose of bourbon, at least a quadruple measure, added a splash of Coke and then stopped.

Okay, I thought, let's do this.

The powder was in the top cabinet, behind packs of organic barley and quinoa that we never use. I unwrapped the plastic and took out the bottle. I put on a pair of wash gloves and carefully unscrewed the lid, catching a faint whiff of something, thick, clotted and musty, like a crypt filled with dead spiders' webs and moths' wings. I took a teaspoon and scooped out a tiny pinch. It was a dull grey colour. Quick, I stirred it in. A brief fizz as it met the JD and Coke, then nothing. I added two ice cubes.

I gave everyone a beer who wanted one and handed the drink to Ben. 'Thanks man,' he said, turning straight back to Mookie. She avoided looking at me. I went and sat back down in the bay window seat. The evening felt almost as hot as the day. Mookie was giving him the full beam.

After everyone had finished their drinks the cars came to take us into Manhattan. I'd been watching Ben, wondering if anything was going to happen and I saw that now he appeared to be very drunk and sleepy. His eyes kept closing and his head was flopping back and forward, his speech wandering – he was telling the same anecdote about the drill sergeant with the prosthetic legs – but less coherently than before and Mookie was nodding in a slightly desperate way and then, when everyone stood to go, he remained in the chair. His head flopped forward.

'What's up with Ben?' said Tao.

'I think he's asleep,' said Mookie.

'Ben, motherfucker! Wake up!' Brock shook his cousin violently. No luck. He slapped the guy in the face – playfully, the first time – harder, the second. 'Out cold.'

'I guess he can't handle his booze,' I ventured.

'Well, we're still going out aren't we?' said Tao.

'He does look sort of pale,' Mookie added. She was right. His healthy tan had drained away, his skin was glassy and he hardly seemed to be breathing.

Fuck, I thought, this is bad. What if the potion was dangerous, like Rich had said? Ben might die. Or Mookie might want to stay and look after him. I didn't know? Perhaps the potion wasn't very strong. He might wake up in a few minutes and then what? I had an idea. 'Look, it's cool,' I said, 'I'm kind of tired anyway and we're home. I'll keep an eye on him. You guys go have fun.'

The others agreed. 'It's sweet of you to look after Ben,' said Mookie, the first thing she had properly said to me all evening. Result.

***

Tao, Joel and Brock helped me carry Ben to his bed. We laid him on top of the duvet. He didn't move. 'Christ, the man is out cold,' said Tao. We all stood over him.

'He'll be fine,' I said. No one else seemed particularly worried, but then they didn't know I'd given him a dose of zombie dust. After the others had gone I took a chair and sat by Ben's bed. He was so pale and his skin felt cold and clammy. I put my ear close to his mouth, wondering if I could detect a faint trace of a breath. Nothing. I picked up one heavy arm and felt for a pulse. Again, nothing.

Okay, I thought, perhaps he was dead. Had I killed him? I felt suddenly very hot with panic and then very cold with fear and then very sober in a 'what have I done' sort of way. From the little I'd read I knew that someone who was made into a zombie appeared to be dead – to the point that a doctor might think they had died – but they were still alive. It was just the appearance of death. I'd never seen a dead body before but I guess Ben looked dead. But was he really dead or did he just look it? I guess I had to wait. As there wasn't much else to do I rolled a spliff, brought my laptop into the bedroom and went on Facebook. I chatted with Sarah for a bit but didn't tell her what was going on. Sometimes I thought it was a lot easier to have a sort of virtual girlfriend. An emoticon conveyed more than an actual smile. Or at least it was a lot simpler.

A horrible scream tore me from my thoughts. Ben. His whole body convulsed, his chest pushing upwards, his fists clenched, pulling at the air like a drowning man trying to grab hold of a rope; he gasped, lips frothing, eyes opened and bulging like two overheated golf balls while a horrible gagging, gasping noise came from inside before his screams diminished into a sound like the last gurgle of water disappearing down the plug.

Well, I thought, at least this meant he wasn't dead.

He slumped back. A sharp smell filled the air. Urgh, silly fucker just pissed himself. He also seemed dead again. I don't know. The whole thing was doing my head in.

***

I was in the jungle. Again. It must be the heat. I was pushing through a mess of hot, wet leaves when something brushed against my neck. I reached back and knocked it to the ground, a spider, a fucking huge golden spider bristling with shiny metallic hairs. Purple eyes looked at me. There were spiders everywhere. I heard myself scream and jolted awake. Fuck! I wasn't in the jungle at all. I was in Brooklyn. I wish I was in the jungle. It all came back to me. What had I done? Sickened, I clambered out of bed. Gone eleven. The A/C unit in my room had stopped, as was its habit when it got really hot. I could sense the intensity of the sun from the fierce glare behind the blinds. I stumbled into the front room. No sign of Brock. His door was open – perhaps he never came home? But the door to the spare room, where Ben was sleeping, remained closed.

I put my ear to the door.

I thought I could hear something, a faint dragging noise. It stopped and then started. Like awkward, shuffling footsteps, like an old man on death row slowly pacing his cell. A jolt of fear ran through me and I felt my testicles contract. If nothing else, I'd poisoned a marine. I decided that whatever happened I mustn't tell Ben what I'd done. He drank too much. Let's just keep it at that.

I knocked loudly. The dragging noise stopped. 'Ben,' I called out, 'you all right mate.' I noticed that I'd acquired a fake cockney twang. My voice does this when I'm nervous. It does it a lot in the States. A bit of 'mockney' and a lot of 'mate' can have quite an effect out here, with these Americans. It depends though. Ben was from Kentucky.

I opened the door.

Ben was standing in the middle of the room. He didn't have any clothes on although his trousers were tangled around his left leg. His head was slumped forward, as if all the strength had drained from his neck while his arms dangled loose by his side.

'Ben mate,' I said.

I didn't want to look at him, naked, but I did. I had no choice. He had impressive shoulders and arms, a six-pack, toned thighs and a great big, dangling cock. Fuck! A dull grumbling noise began to resonate from somewhere in his throat and his head jerked up. One of his eyes was puffy and closed and the other rolled around without purpose. A spasm twitched his limbs as though he were being manipulated by a drunken puppeteer.

'You had quite a lot to drink mate. How are you feeling?'

He made a noise like grrrnghghghghhhh and began to yank at his cock.

'Mate. Please don't do that.'

He took no notice, doggedly tugging at his member. Almost immediately he was hard. and I mean pornstar cock hard – it was huge, bulging and throbbing, the circumcised head reminding me of the monster mouth in *Aliens* – the little one that pops out of the big mouth and he continued to yank away, a dull grunting noise escaping his lips. Outside of porn I'd never actually seen an erect penis before apart from my own. His fearsome cock twitched and something hot and sticky landed on my arm.

'Jesus fucking Christ Ben!' I jumped like I'd been electrocuted. There it was on my arm! A hot blob of Ben's cum!

Christ! I ran to the kitchen and put my arm under the tap. I washed it off and went back to check on him. Ben was standing in the middle of room, his penis erect but his head and arms hanging down slack.

'Good trick mate,' I tried to laugh. 'You got me.'

Ben didn't move.

'Are you okay?' I said again. 'You're... you're not a zombie, are you?'

A stalactite of drool dangled from his open mouth.

'You're just hungover mate,' I joked. 'You really were knocking them back last night. Don't you remember?'

The stalactite broke, the mucous droplet plopping to the floor. 'Burghhh...' he mumbled. 'Burrnghhhhhh.'

At least his erection appeared to be diminishing. 'Come on then,' I clapped my hands together. 'Let's get you dressed.'

***

Turned out zombie-Ben wasn't all that different from normal Ben. The drool was a tad off-putting and he had trouble with complete sentences, but that aside I didn't think the difference was too noticeable. When Brock came back we were both on the sofa, drinking Diet Cokes and watching Fox News. Some weird shit was going down in North Dakota. A small town had been sealed off by the authorities. No one seemed to know what was happening and the news kept replaying images of scary looking police with gas masks and machine guns blocking the main road in. This was something I loved about the States: the impending sense of apocalypse, the fact that the world was always about to end. I also loved the fact that this calamity was something half the nation seemed to want to happen. None of this English keep calm and carry on bullshit.

'Hey,' said Brock.

'Hey,' I said.

'Grnghghghghh!' said Ben.

Brock did a quick double take. 'Glad you're up,' he took his glasses off and squinted at Ben, who was gazing vacantly at his big toe. 'You okay man?'

'He's got a massive hangover,' I said.

'Mrghhhhhurgh!' said Ben. 'Head...' he mashed a fist into his left eye.

'What the hell is going on there?' Brock gazed at the screen with incomprehension.

'Fuck knows,' I said.

'Taliban,' Ben mumbled. 'Kill.'

***

Living with a zombie was no big deal. Brock didn't seem to notice and Ben was docile enough, most of the time. He'd have these lucid periods when he seemed almost entirely normal, broken with occasional fits of terrible, unearthly screaming. These could, I admit, be distressing until I discovered that putting a scarf or small towel over his face – especially over the eyes – caused him to immediately cease and slump. I think you can do a similar trick with a parrot or other birds. 'I've heard you can get post-traumatic stress disorder before anything happens,' I said to Brock. 'It's called pre-traumatic stress disorder, stress in anticipation of the bad things you know are likely to happen to you.'

'Sure,' said Brock, 'I read about it in *Triple Canopy*.'

Ben was next to us on the sofa, slumped, Colette's scarf wrapped around his face.

'It's impressive,' Colette helped herself to an olive from the bowl on the coffee table. She was opposite, in the easy chair. 'He's so strong and yet so sensitive.'

I pondered whether I should mention the drool. Brock said the rest of the gang was coming over soon so I removed the scarf from Ben. He blinked several times, yawned and fixed a rather sullen gaze on Colette. He slouched and spread his legs so wide that I was forced to sit narrow and upright. 'I'm gonna get me some,' he mumbled.

An hour or so later we were joined by Joel, Tao and Mookie. Tao had some coke. We did lines off a mirror. Ben did some too. It seemed to brighten him up, or maybe it just seemed that way, I don't know. Mookie was looking good in a short red dress. I'd always thought of her as quite pale, but her legs had turned the colour of salted caramel in the sun. I missed those legs.

After that, things got a bit messed up for a while. We finished the coke and went down to a bar on the corner. 'Shots,' said Ben. 'Get me.' He bought tequila shots for everybody. We did those, then we did some more, then we had beers. Tao called his dealer for more coke. It was midnight. Joel said he was tired and headed home but the rest of us went back to the flat.

Brock put on some tunes and everybody started shouting at the same time. 'Music!' bellowed Ben and he pulled off his T-shirt, much to the delight of the girls. I'd been trying to engage Mookie a couple of times in the evening and while she hadn't exactly been off with me, she'd hardly been on.

'Brock,' it was a struggle to make myself heard over the Beastie Boys classic 'Sabotage', 'Do you know what the hell is up with Mookie?'

'She still pissed at you for the Sarah thing?'

'Yeah, I mean, I guess so. What's her problem?'

'Do you like her?'

'Yeah, well, sort of.'

'I think she thinks you don't like her.'

'No.'

'You don't want to like her bro, she's a waste of time, I'm telling you. Anyway, look,' he pointed at Ben, who was sort of head banging to the music in the corner. Mookie went over to join him. 'I think she likes Ben.'

'That's what I'm worried about.'

'Dude, come on,' Brock slapped me playfully on the arm. 'He's going back to base tomorrow. He's in Afghanistan by Tuesday. He might die out there. Who cares what he does tonight?'

'I guess.' I saw his point, but at the same time it didn't exactly seem fair.

'Mookie's a fucking mess anyway dude, especially when she's been doing coke. Don't worry about it.'

But I did worry about it. I could see what was going to happen. Anyone could.

I did more coke with Tao. 'Slow down man,' he said.

'Word,' I said, snorting it up.

'Word?'

'I'm fine. Leave me alone.'

The music changed. Now Mookie and Ben were doing some sort of slow dance. A zombie bump 'n' grind. A slow jam from the dead. Fuck it. Mookie turned around and was dancing with her back pressed against Ben's chest, her bum rubbing against his groin, their heads almost touching. She touched the side of his head and they moved together, cheek to cheek. She didn't seem to notice the drool. 'Fucking look at that,' I muttered although no one else heard me. I just knew what was going to happen. Ben was going to pound her with his massive exploding zombie cock.

I got up. Whoah... bit of a head rush. Took a moment to get my bearings. 'Hey,' I announced, 'I'm going to the kitchen. Can I fix anyone a drink?'

It turned out everyone wanted a drink. How about that?

In the kitchen I got out the vodka.

Then I opened the cupboard and reached for the vial stashed away at the back. Time, I decided, for everyone to have a go.

POUR OUT THE VIALS

Quiet at last so I decide to slip from my room and risk a look. I knew Daddy had gone off to an all-night revival. Earlier, Mom was also full of the Holy Spirit as well as another sort of spirit, guzzling vodka from the bottle and calling on the Lord Jesus to do this and that, cleanse our sins and strike down the abortion doctors and evolutionists, all the usual. But she'd been quiet for the last half hour so I figured she must have zonked out by now. I'm right: there she is, sprawled on the sofa, mouth open, snoring away. I scan the area to check to make sure she hasn't left any cigarettes burning – the last thing we need is her setting fire to the new sofa like she did with the old – then I go over to her laptop.

She's left it open and, as I suspected, she's been online reading the *NewOathKeepers* blogspot again. I squeeze next to her slumbering body and take a look at what Earl's got to say for himself. He updated the blog a couple of hours ago with new text and a number of embedded videos. It's risky, doing this: Mom would go ape-shit if she found out I knew about Earl. Her breathing is rather laboured, a sort of ropey wheeze but I don't think I'm going to disturb her. She's too far gone.

I start to read:

Fellow Patriots!
Below we have a number of video files recovered from a camcorder belonging to Jennifer Fairweather, a student from Cornell University. As far as I understand, Fairweather is part of a scientific research team from Cornell sent to Stanley in North Dakota at the bequest of the oil industry to investigate new sinkholes that may or may not have been caused by extensive fracking in the area. At present the whereabouts of Jennifer Fairweather and other members of the research team remain unknown. The footage is directly connected to events we believe have led to the recent quarantining of the town by the Feds.

I was given the footage by one of my contacts at the FBI. He told me they found the camcorder on the outskirts of Stanley. Regular readers will know that for a long time I've been suspicious of this so-called 'fracking'. Are these companies really extracting oil from the earth or is it, in fact, another diabolical strategy by the New World Order to poison and control us all?

These events remind us of the importance of our sacred oath and our promise to uphold the

Constitution and defend our fellow Americans against the tyranny of unjust laws and the infringement of our freedoms. In this instance the New World Order are going beyond the bounds to threaten us, to threaten our children, our children's children and everything that makes America a great nation. It seems to me, fellow patriots, that this footage is the strongest evidence yet that the conspiracy involves not only the Federal Government and US Military, but also the state government of North Dakota, Exxon, Chevron Mobile and other corporations involved in oil extraction operations and their Illuminati backers. Watch the footage and judge for yourself. Behold the madness and disease that smites these so-called scientists.

It's like the Book of Revelation says, 'I heard a great voice out of the temple saying to the seven angels, Go your ways, and pour out the vials of the wrath of God upon the earth. And the first went, and poured out his vial upon the earth; and there fell a noisome and grievous sore upon the men which had the mark of the beast, and *upon* them which worshipped his image.' Watch the videos and behold as Revelation is fulfilled. Yea, my friends, patriots and true believers, watch and repent if you have not done so, for a mighty judgement shall fall on us all.

My fellow Oath Keepers will be well aware that in my commitment to the truth, I've faced many threats. I've said it before and let me say again, I'd rather die a free man in the light of the truth than be a slave languishing in darkness! Illuminati might mean light, but the secretive activities of our nefarious leaders cast a long shadow over the so-called free world. Our forefathers stood up against tyranny in defence of liberty – we must follow their example. I have my rifle and my Bible by my side: let them come, I say, let them come.

Yours, as ever

Earl Landis

The usual fuss and bluster. Some of Earl's blog is so badly written it's actually embarrassing. I mean, I figure I could do better and I'm fifteen. I get the sense he's never really sure what he's on about. Illuminati, New World Order, Book of Revelation, blah, blah, blah. All the same, I scroll to the first video file, press play and then immediately pause it, forgetting to put my headphones on and worried in case the audio wakes Mom.

I go back to my room and fetch my headphones. As I do so, I hear Mom in my head, as always. 'Esther,' she says, 'it's like what's written in the good book. The devil makes work for idle hands so don't you go concerning yourself with things that's not your business.' That's Mom though, always making stuff up and pretending it's in the Bible as if that's going to win the argument. My mom has never even read the whole Bible.

I've been stuck at home for so long now I'm going mad with boredom. Nearly a year since Daddy had the 'incident' in Disney World and lost his job, eight months since they pulled me out of school, three months since we went any further than the church which is just eight blocks away. We don't even go out shopping anymore. Mom gets it all delivered online. Everything out there is 'corrupt' according to her, but I just see a street lined with bungalows identical to the one we live in. Mom goes on about how the neighbourhood has gone 'downhill' and keeps saying we need to move to a more righteous place but I don't know if we're ever going anywhere. I worry I might be stuck here for good.

I guess I can at least watch the videos and imagine I'm visiting Dakota. I do remember something in the news a few weeks ago about an outbreak of a mysterious illness up there – Fox got all excited for a day or two that it might be Ebola – but I don't know what happened to the story. It disappeared, like stories do. Nothing really seems to connect or continue anymore – it's like things start and things finish and other stuff happens in between and none of it makes sense. I turn on the TV one day and there'll be a revolution in some country in the Middle East and everybody's happy about it, the people are taking their freedoms, they want democracy, then a week later I turn on the TV and we're dropping bombs on the same people we were supporting just before. Or I'll see that some city mayor or governor is being indicted for fraud or got caught out with crack and paying prostitutes to urinate all over them and the next thing I see they're on the TV again, running for something or other and everyone's cheering. I try to pay close attention – what else can I do? But all the connections are broken. Nothing makes sense. There is the law but it doesn't stand up the same for everyone. Some people murder and go scot-free. Some people get put away for crimes they didn't even commit. Above that, according to Mom, there's God's law but I don't see God doing much to help anybody, least of all us.

Mom is still out of it. I see she drank most of the bottle. I roll it under the coffee table, where it joins the others. The house is filthy – Mom never does anything, Dad's always at church, it's just me. I've cleaned up once or twice but right after I finish Mom has the place half back to where it was before. So I lock myself in my room and read history books. No school and Mom has banned my friends from coming over, says they haven't been 'saved'. I keep thinking about sneaking out but it's too far to walk anywhere. 'Why do you have to ruin my life?' I whisper at Mom. I know I shouldn't but sometimes I really do hate her ugly stupid face. A slither of drool escapes from the side of her mouth and trickles down her cheek.

Okay. I take a deep breath, sit down and plug in my headphones.

I start the first video file. It's hard to work out what's going on, the camera jerks around before I see a chubby woman who I guess is in her mid-twenties, with glasses and short blonde hair. She checks the camera is working, then sits down on a bed. She's wearing a fleece and jeans and must be in a hotel room. 'So we finally made it,' she says. 'It's been a long and tiring day. I've never been to the Dakotas before and this is likely to be our last night in civilisation for quite some time. Tomorrow we're going to the site to look at this.' She holds up a photograph of a huge black hole, surprisingly even in shape, a black disc against the reddish ground. 'Sinkholes. Lots of them. Professor Dyer says the largest are more than sixty feet wide, perhaps bigger. How deep it goes, at this stage, nobody knows. Dyer says that dozens of new holes have been reported in the last three weeks alone—'

She's interrupted when the door to her room opens and a young man appears. 'Jenny, come and take a look at this.'

Jennifer picks up the camera. There's a brief interlude as she goes outside. It's dark but the camera tries to focus on a bright light in the sky that seems to hover for a moment before flaring up and burning out. 'Oh my God,' says Jennifer. 'What an amazing shooting star.'

'The sky is so clear out here, it's incredible,' says another voice. Then the footage cuts out.

That seems to be it for the first video file.

I get up and drink a glass of water. Mom mumbles something in her sleep. 'Oh shut up Mom,' I whisper at her, clicking on the second.

In this one Jennifer is sitting close to the camera, wearing a woolly hat pulled right down over her ears. It's windy – I think she's in a tent – and it's difficult to make out what she's saying. She says something about how hard it was to get there and that the weather is 'awful'. Then the screen starts to blur and break up with static. Someone else in the tent is speaking to her but I can't hear a word. The footage ends.

I sort of wonder whether it's worth continuing with the files. Ever since I discovered Mom was having a secret correspondence with Earl, I've been keeping an eye on his blog and it's mostly just ridiculous conspiracy theories. For example, someone will report that the army is doing an exercise in Texas and send him photos of some tanks on the highway and he'll start posting about Texas being 'invaded' and 'occupied'. If anything like this really did happen I reckon he would run a mile but until then I'd say Earl is enjoying his fantasies.

Whatever. I click on the third file.

The camera footage is very wobbly and seems to be looking at a large hole. It pulls back to reveal a number of people standing at the edge. It's windy and the wind makes it hard to hear what's going on but I can just about make out several voices, in English and Spanish. The camera turns to a middle-aged guy with a big beard wearing an orange windbreaker. 'This would appear to be the largest of the holes,' he's having to shout. 'We're calling it Big Mac for the time being. We are approximately one point five miles north, north-west from the campsite. As you can see—' the wind drowns him out for a moment, '... There are several other sinkholes close to here although we think the others are smaller. What's surprising is that this is a new hole. It's not on the recent satellite photos which would suggest it appeared in the last sixty-four hours or so.' The camera pans around to show a dozen or so individuals, mostly wrapped up against the wind with scarves, hoods and sunglasses. The camera advances close to the edge. Another man, wearing a protective suit and a helmet mounted with a torch and a GoPro camera is strapping himself into a safety harness. Men are preparing to lower him into the hole. The film cuts out.

Okay, I admit I'm intrigued. This is better than Earl's usual crap. I can see why people are worried about fracking. Carly sent me a video about it on Facebook –

showing how they pump tons of chemicals deep into the earth and how it can poison the water supply, even cause earthquakes and even if that's not true, it doesn't sound good. The funny thing is my parents don't usually give a damn about these issues. Mom likes to quote Sarah Palin saying God put everything in the earth for us to use. Elsewhere on the blog I've seen Earl call global warming a hoax and another attempt by the 'Illuminati' to control us and tell us what we can and can't do. All I know is each year is hotter than the last and every hurricane season more fearsome than the one before.

I watch the next file.

We're in a larger tent. The guy with the beard is standing at the front, talking. 'So, team, it looks like "Big Mac" drops about eighty-five feet, the hole remaining remarkably consistent in terms of circumference all the way down to a mound of displaced top soil – again suggesting that it opened up recently. Dr Schaffer's exploration,' and he gestures at the guy standing next to him, 'would suggest there are numerous small crevices and off-shoots leading away from the main vault. Furthermore, the sides of the hole are unusually smooth. I've seen plenty of much larger holes than this, but for one to open up so suddenly and for so many to appear in such a short space of time is most peculiar—' Mom stirs, mumbling and shifting slightly on the sofa, one of her feet pushing against me. 'Fucking load of shit,' she mumbles to herself. 'We wouldn't expect,' the professor continues, 'this type of cover collapse hole to emerge here, not like this and not unless the fracking activities have had a very extreme effect on the water table—' His voice is drowned out by the wind, which shakes the tent, a continuous and dramatic howling. The camera cuts out.

Okay. Next one.

I can't see anything. Just darkness and the sound of heavy, anxious breathing. Then a voice – Jennifer – speaking while she seems to be walking about in the dark. 'What a terrible nightmare,' she says. 'At least that awful wind has stopped. Gosh, it's so dark and quiet. I've never had a dream like that before... There were... Thousands of people – slaves, I think – building some sort of huge... I don't know, like a pyramid or a ziggurat or something in a waste of dust and there was a thing at the top, like an altar, and they kept taking the slaves, kept draining their blood leaving behind a pile of corpses, just empty husks of skin, hollow bodies discarded like old clothes. I had to get up. It freaked me right out. It's weird out here. I don't know... I'm not usually like this. And William is being off with me. I'm worried I've done something wrong. I guess he's just preoccupied—'

'¿Quién es? ¿Qué pasa?' The voice interrupts her musings.

'Wait, it's just me. Jennifer. Is that you Miguel?'

The video cuts out.

I get up to go to the bathroom and wander around the house. I open the front door and stand looking at the street. It's late and very quiet. I can just imagine Daddy in church, singing and swaying, arms raised, eyes closed, face filled with beatific grace. If only. And wow, it's so humid, even for Florida, like stepping into a giant sauna. The weatherman keeps saying a storm is coming, but it never does.

The next video file is the most interesting. We seem to be back in a tent and I can hear Jennifer whisper, 'I guess

I shouldn't be filming this, but look what we found in that hole.' The camera zooms in on a number of objects that have been placed on a sheet of orange tarpaulin. A dozen or so specimens. Some just fragments varying in size but a couple appear more or less whole. They are a dull, greyish colour although it's difficult to tell how much of that might be due to dirt. My guess is that they are carved out of stone but then for all I can tell they could be made of plastic or bone. As the camera zooms closer it's clear that some of the fragments are decorated with fine carvings. Intricate, spider-web patterns are faintly visible on the surface of some of the fragments. The camera pans over the two most intact objects, figurines about the size of a Barbie doll. They are humanoid in shape but with unusually large heads that look as if they end in tentacles, as if the head of an octopus type creature had been grafted onto a humanoid body. Even with the dirt and obvious erosion, the figures look as though they have been expertly crafted and are also covered in finely wrought swirls, waves and parallel lines.

'What are you doing Jenny?' says another voice. It's the guy who interrupted her on the first file.

'I wanted to get them on film.'

'William will be furious if he sees you doing this.'

'Oh come on? This is important.'

'I know it's important. That's why you shouldn't be recording this for your video diary.'

'What do you think they are made of?' I see her hand reaching down to pick one up. 'They're really, really heavy.'

'I know! Put them down. Christ, you shouldn't touch them. William says he's calling in his friend Professor

Coxworth-Grove to have a look. We just have to sit tight 'til then. He's been saying this might be the most important discovery since Tutankhamun's tomb.'

'I think they're made of metal. Some sort of iron?'

'I guess.'

'It's weird, I mean, the Native American tribes never had the technology to make this sort of thing.'

'Right.'

Jennifer puts down the figurine. 'I'm so itchy... Look.' The camera jolts about a bit before focusing on her exposed arm, the skin marked with red welts.

'Me too,' says the guy, 'I'm itching like a fucking dog. Schaffer was saying he thinks there might be ticks in the long grass.'

'Oh great. Like we're all going to get Lyme disease. Perfect.'

'You had better turn that off.'

The footage ends.

I admit, those figurines did look really weird.

Next file. The camera is pointing at the ground, but I can hear voices. I recognise the professor, William Dyer, who seems to be having an argument with a man with a Hispanic accent. 'Listen Rodriguez, you and your crew have been paid to do a job,' he's saying. 'We need you on site.'

'*Señor*, I tell you, the men will not work.'

'What do you mean? You get your lazy goddam Mexican asses—'

'William,' Jennifer interrupts, 'Rodriguez and his men are from Guatemala.'

'*Si, Guatemala señor.*'

'Do I look like I give a damn where you're from? This might be the most important discovery in the last hundred years of archaeology and you're refusing to work because... because?'

'*Señor*, this is not a good place. You are ill. Your students are ill. This is not a place for man. Some things should be left for God, *comprende*?'

'No, you *comprende* this Rodriguez. You get your men back in that hole and continue with the excavations otherwise I'll have your ass shipped home before you can say – wait, Jennifer, you're not filming this are you?'

'Me? No. Oh, shit, sorry, I left it on.' The camera cuts out.

Just two files left. A quick check on Mom but she's snoring away. Okay. The footage in the next is very, very wobbly, as if the person with the camera is running. They're outside in a dust storm and the air is thick with orange haze. The camera jiggles a bit but then focuses on a figure standing some distance away and he's – wait, is he... My goodness, yes he is, he's naked and his skin is red with some sort of rash. Scattered about on the ground are various items of clothing that must have been discarded in haste – as if he ran out into the storm, ripping off his clothes as he went. As the camera gets closer, I can see the man has opened his arms wide to the sky, as if to embrace the wind and the rash – ew, gross – it's like his skin has been flayed off or turned transparent and... is that? Can I see the blood pumping through his body. Is that...? But then the camera turns around and I can see a number of others, recognisable from earlier footage, all standing in the wind and pulling off their clothes too and their skin is also horribly red, like they've been dipped in scalding hot water... The camera drops to the floor and I can't see anything, just the sound of the wind and someone shouting something that sounds like 'Ithooca! Ithooca!'

Right. I'm not sure what to make of that.

One more file left. I'm about to click on it when I hear the sound of a car pulling up. Headlights flash through the closed curtains. I shut the laptop and leap up, running to the window.

Shit! Daddy's back. The revival must have finished early.

Mom jolts up like she's been zapped with ten thousand vaults. 'ESTHER!' she shouts 'ESTHER WHERE THE HELL ARE YOU?'

I duck down so she can't see me and quick as possible crawl along the corridor to my bedroom. I shut the door, kill the lights, dive under the covers and pretend to be asleep.

THE KISS OF THE NEPHILIM

Two-thirty in the morning, a Tuesday morning I think and I'm sitting in a 24-hour Taco Bell in Miami Beach waiting for a fat Cuban whore called Esmeralda to score some crack. She's only been gone five minutes and said it would probably take thirty. Who knows, that could mean an hour, maybe longer? At least I haven't given her any money. She's been 'incentivised', as others might say, to return. Or perhaps she'll smoke it all herself and forget about me? Somehow, I doubt that. Still, here I am, picking over the remains of a 'Nacho cheese Doritos Locos Tacos Supreme' and I have to ask myself: how do I end up in these situations? It's really quite unfortunate, squalid and embarrassing, but I'm on the run. I'm hiding out. Rumour has it there's a safe house for my kind somewhere in the Miami Beach area and I'm trying to make contact. I left a message on a chat room that purports to be for us and those who support us. So far, no response. The whole thing might be fake anyway. We're so alone these days, that's the trouble, and with so few of us left we have to keep a low profile. It's not like it used to be. But this time I've only myself to blame. I was indiscreet. My appetites got the better of me.

I wonder what I'll do with Esmeralda after we've smoked some rock? If we're just going to fuck we can go back to my hotel a couple of blocks away. I'm tempted to do more but for that we need to go somewhere quiet. Her place, if she lives alone... But no, I shouldn't. I tell myself to leave it. She's probably got kids or lives with someone and besides, giving in only makes it worse, it inflames the desire, the red, restless rage. I need to stop, need to calm down. 'Restraint,' as my old master used to say, 'is what really separates us from them.'

'Hey honey.' To my surprise, Esmeralda is back. She shows me the rocks in her hand and then slips the tiny parcel into the small gap between her tight yellow top and enormous breasts.

'My hotel is close, if you want to go.'

'Sure thing baby.'

We got back to my hotel – well, a motel really – with faux Deco stylings. Esmeralda takes off her heels and groans with relief as she sits on the bed. 'Christ, my toes are killing me.' I try not to look at her feet, covered in blisters from her shoes, or her red chipped nails. She produces a small glass pipe and lighter from her fake Versace handbag.

We smoke some rocks. She coughs a lot but my head just goes warm and I feel my body tingle.

'Good huh?'

'Yeah.' It's nothing, a little crack, whatever. It hits and for a second or two I feel good, the drug spurring a dormant memory, past images that glide across my mind, the drone of insects merging with the songs of the slaves in the cotton field, beautiful hymns to their useless God while I sit in the shade, dazed by the summer heat, a mint julep in my hand...

'You want some of this now, huh? You ready?'

'Yeah.'

She takes off her top and unclips her bra. 'Like that? You want it this way?'

'Yeah.'

'That good. You like that?'

' _ '

'Yeah, that's right honey. My, you're a big one aren't you? There we go.'

'Yeah.'

'There we go.'

'Urgh.'

'That's right honey, that's good.'

She lets me go and wipes her breasts with a tissue. I lie back on the bed, we smoke more crack and I tell Esmeralda a few stories. Her eyes get glassy and she laughs too hard. Soon enough it's light outside. 'Well,' I say to her, 'it's morning. I guess you ought to be getting along.'

'Oh, you're a pretty boy.'

'Fun huh?' She puts her clothes back on. 'You've got some money right?'

She nods.

'Leave it for me, won't you?' She nods her head as if a little confused by what I'm asking.

'All of it?'

'Yep, all of it.'

She rummages through her bag and takes out about two hundred dollars. 'Thanks sweetheart,' I give her a kiss on the lips and wave her goodbye. If she remembers anything, she'll put it down to being high. Weak-minded fool. I open the blinds. The brightness is toxic so I close them again and add the cash to my wallet. I shower then lie on the bed watching Fox News looking to see if the media picked up on what happened in Atlanta but nothing. Just the thought of that child gets my juices flowing... According to Fox a big hurricane is coming this way, Hurricane Harker, and the headlines are dominated by storm warnings, footage of the state governor urging people further upstate to evacuate 'low-lying coastal areas'. I love Fox News. Seven-thirty a.m. Still too early to check in with Angela, my therapist, much as I want to tell her what's been happening. I don't need another lecture about 'boundaries' again.

What to do? I get very bored, you see. Very bored indeed. I turn off the TV and log onto *YouthTube*, curious to catch up on Kimberly. Things haven't been going so well for her lately. Like most of the kids on *YouthTube* she started off with hopes of being a singer or an actress, maybe a model. I'm not even sure what it is about her that caught my attention, after all *YouthTube* is full of much hotter, much younger, much more talented kids. Perhaps it was her very homeliness that appealed to me, the cute homemade videos of her singing her squeaky pop songs. Tasteful, if amateurish bikini and lingerie shots in 'aspirational' locations, the occasional slight risqué pose giving a hint of nipple or revealing just enough to imagine what her pussy looks like. Shaven, I reckon, like all the girls out there these days. But that was then and this is now. I guess it didn't happen for her: the hoped-for sponsorships didn't come through: not enough hits, not enough donations, no fashion deal, no record deal, no modelling contract, no auditions. Would I pay money to watch her lip-synching to some brat-pop? No, no I wouldn't. So now she's in the same deep shit as half the kids on *YouthTube*. She's crossed over, making black and red vids. Will I pay to watch her get fucked? I will. A new video is up: $2 to access Kimberly's first 'anal adventure'. I press the donate button. In the seven-minute film a dude wearing a leather mask gives it to her but the whole thing depresses me. Is this how bad it's got for kids? Sure, a handful have become rich and 'hyper-visible' through *YouthTube*, but the majority end up like Kimberly with a cock up their ass. Afterwards, she smiles at the camera (the smile looks strained, if I'm honest, I think she's in a lot of pain) and she says, 'If I reach my target of $10,000 you can watch me get fucked by two guys next time.' The counter at the bottom of the screen reads $8,376.

I log off. The world is nothing but a pyramid of cruelty, violence and exploitation and for this reason it's best to be on top. I used to be at the top, the very top. Not any more. The hunter turns hunted. I know this is what Angela calls 'my white man's rage' the result, according to her, of my resentment towards feminism, multi-culturalism, liberalism, civil rights for homosexuals and African-Americans and migrants and the overall 'de-centering of privileged white male subjectivity' as she puts it, but then her eyes just glaze over when I try and tell her what it was really like, back on the plantation, an army of black bucks to bend to my will.

Okay. Time to go out.

Miami in September. It's like being stuck under a fat girl's armpit. The vilest season. An overcast sky, hazy and grey with a smoggy sort of mist. No wind, just a suffocating, sticky heat. The beach is quiet, a few muscle nuts and queers busting weights, the odd dog walker. Two women jog slowly past, water bottles in hand. I admire their departing asses and spend a while staring at the flat grey sea. I hate this city, the antithesis of all I stand for. Christ alive, the US has gone to the dogs. I would never come here if not for the safe house.

After a while the sun starts to break through, peeling away the cloud and the sky underneath is a relentless blue, the brilliant light bleaching everything, flattening the streets, sucking up the shadows. No sign of any storm, not even a hint. People hide indoors behind tinted windows. I go back to the hotel. 'What's this about the storm?' I ask the guy on reception but he just shrugs. Stupid fucking wetback probably doesn't speak English.

I log onto the chat room.

What's this? My message has been answered! Someone has written:

And there will not be left any man that eateth blood or that sheddeth the blood of man on the earth, nor will there be left to him any seed or descendants living under heaven; for into Sheol will they go and into the place of condemnation will they descend. And into the darkness of the deep will they all be removed by a violent death.

An interesting response. Posted by Elioud-Follower25, three hours ago. I hesitate for a minute or two, wondering if I should leave it. But if I do, what next? I'm still homeless and funds are running low. How many times in a life can one start again? I send them a private message 'Where r u?' and my cell number.

Ten minutes later my phone buzzes. A link to a location on Google maps. A parking lot five blocks away. A text arrives. *Be there in an hour. I'll be in a black Prius, California plates.*

'Okay' I text back.

***

An hour later and I'm there. It's fiercely hot now and I'm smothered in sunblock. The lot is largely empty, the Prius parked back in the shade of a high wall and dwarfed by the enormous SUV next to it. I keep my eyes open as I approach, looking this way, looking that, but the streets are devoid of pedestrians. I'm carrying a bag with a change of clothes, toothbrush and my 9mm Glock, just to be sure. I hesitate but the front door of the Prius opens and I get in. The guy in the driver's seat is a pasty, weedy looking little dude, deathly pale and sweating despite the A/C. He's clearly nervous, a little jittery, round glasses with blue filters covering his eyes like two moons as his head bobs up and down. There's a thin scarf around his neck and he's wearing a long, black leather coat. Another Goth (they always are), even down to the stupid Celtic-style rings adorning his fingers.

'Elioud-Follower?' I say.

'You can call me Colin.'

'Steve,' I say.

'I...' the guy swallows, 'I'm pleased to meet you.'

'Thank you for answering. I was beginning to wonder—'

'—I'm sorry,' he cuts in, clearly nervous. 'But I have to ask. There are some tests, you see. Questions. I need to know the answers before we can proceed.'

'Go on.'

'You need to tell me your given name. The one bequeathed to you.'

I sigh. 'I've not uttered this name in a long time.'

His voice drops to a whisper, 'But I can't take you to Sanctuary otherwise. You might not be who you say you are.'

'Seriously?'

'We have a lot of pretenders. A lot of wannabes. You'd be surprised.'

'Fine.' I clear my throat. 'My given name is Aretstikapha, that is to say Aretstikapha of Hartford, which is where I was born. Hartford, Connecticut. In 1793. I was a New England boy, originally. This name comes from those who watch over us, those who were there at the beginning and who shall return at the end, the Archon, the true rulers and Lords of the Universe. The name was given to me by the one who calls himself Arâkîba, a corruption of his master's name as he was a corruption of his master and as I too am a corruption of this original seed.'

'Where is this Arâkîba now?'

'I've no idea.' I shrug. 'Banished to the outer dark. Or possibly operating as a realtor in the Des Moines area.' Colin doesn't appreciate my attempt at humour. 'Put it this way. He doesn't send me postcards. I haven't seen him since oh...' I scratch my nose, 'just after the Civil War.'

'He left you?'

'Eventually. Why wouldn't he? What am I anyway? A Quarter-blood of no particular merit. He must have bequeathed hundreds, perhaps thousands of us, if you think about it, across the millennia. I mean, we can't even really begin to imagine...'

Colin nods, tapping into his phone. 'There is just one more test,' he says. 'The final, absolute proof.'

'What?'

His quivering fingers remove the scarf. Quite far down, on the left side of his neck, is a bandage. Wincing, he peels it off to reveal an angry red mark, like the mother of all lovebites. Two puncture marks are visible in the centre, tipped with red crusted scabs.

'You can't be serious?'

'Oh yes,' he whispers, 'I am very serious.' It's tempting, the sight of it, his open, vulnerable neck, the skin so soft and all that blood, just underneath, torrents of crimson life pumping through throbbing veins. The memory of the child comes back and I feel it, an ache that starts in my jaw and my teeth and stretches all the way down to my spine, my stomach, even my cock.

'Are you sure you want me to?' I ask, my voice caught tight in my throat.

'Oh yes...' he sighs.

'What if I can't control myself?' It seems only fair to warn him.

'Well then...' he says dismissively. Is that a hint of a smile on his face? '...If that happens you'll be stuck here. Without Sanctuary. You'll never find it and the police will arrest you for murder.'

'They haven't yet,' I say, leaning in. I place my mouth over the wound. I can feel him with my mouth, his heart pulsing between my teeth: a shudder and there is a sensation of intense internal pressure and relief as my teeth stretch and extend before punctuating his skin like two plaque inflected needles. First taste and it's always intoxicating, the rush of it, his life force surging into me. I sup at his vital essence. But careful... I must be careful, I must not go too far, must not kill the man, not take it all from him, even as I drink, even as images tumble through my mind – memories of my old master, of the time he leant in, the time his fangs broke my neck with a shiver of sweet ecstasy, that and the ziggurat in the badlands, the red waste, a sea of blood... so I break away, gasping like a diver, head spinning, wiping the crimson stain from my lips while Colin, I notice, sinks back in his seat, only the whites of his eyes visible and he moans softly, a single trail of blood trickling down his neck. I also see that he has his cock out and is frantically pulling at himself. *Urgh*, I should have known he'd be one of those types.

'Don't stop,' he gasps. Then, 'You stopped.'

'I had to.' I'm not sure where to look so I look outside. 'Can you put your penis away?' I ask nicely.

'You can't... I mean, you are not able to make me?'

'What?'

'Like you! One of you. You can't make me a vampire?'

'No! Jesus. I don't have that power. No one does anymore. I'm just a Quarter-blood. Those who could...'

'The Watchers are all sleeping,' he says, whimpering with a sudden melancholy.

'Or dead,' I add. I guess the guy can't help himself. He must be experiencing a tiny fraction of what I went through when I met my Master or when He chose me, the sweet blissful oblivion of a kiss from the Nephilim.

There's nothing else like it. 'And don't call me a vampire,' I snap, perhaps more annoyed by his use of the word than I should be. 'This isn't some Hollywood production.'

'Master,' he nods, bowing his head and zipping his fly.

'Take me to Sanctuary,' I command and he starts the engine.

***

'You're not a vampire,' Angela would say while I lay on her couch cuddling one of the soft toys she liked to provide for 'tactile comfort'. 'And,' she would continue, 'you're certainly not two hundred and fifty years old. You might think you are, but you're not.'

'Two hundred and fifty years is nothing,' I tried to explain. 'My Master was more than three thousand years old. He witnessed the genocide of the Aztecs. He was there. And his Master was one of the Old Ones, one of the First Men, the Watchers at the End of Time. His Master was not of this Earth. His Master came to this Earth fifty thousand years ago and was already immeasurably old, even then. Two hundred and fifty years is nothing. I'm a baby. Would you like me tell you about life in 1800? About the house where I was born?'

'Go on then,' Angela would say, doing her best (I could tell) not to sound bored, 'Tell me about the 1800s,' and I would try although – to be honest – it was all so long ago I struggle to remember much and she was right when she used to respond, 'You could have got all this from a book.'

'You don't understand,' our discussions went around like this, 'once I had a plantation with ten thousand acres and three hundred slaves at my command. The finest niggers money could buy—'

'—African-Americans, please.'

'Whatever.'

'Steve, we have spoken about your use of inappropriate and racially offensive language.'

Whenever she did this I would get vexed and start to shout, 'They were my niggers, niggers I tell you. Mine! To fuck, to kill, to suck their blood, to do with as I chose. All of them, three hundred niggers, subservient to me, to my will.'

'Tell me more about these feelings of power, this assumption of superiority you seem to enjoy—'

'—Enjoy, I don't enjoy anything! What does enjoyment have to do with it?'

'How long have you had these feelings?'

'I've told you. More than two hundred years. Ever since my Master, a Half-blood, made me into one of them.'

'A vampire, you say?'

'We prefer the term Nephilim.'

'Half man, half angel?'

'I wouldn't recognise the word angel. They're not angels. God didn't make us.'

'Why do you reject the word vampire? It's not accurate?'

'Well, look, in the sense that I drink human blood, yes it is. We all do. But it was my Master who gave me eternal life, if you want to call it that.'

'Eternal life?'

They were frustrating, these discussions. I only saw my therapist to make sure the doctor continued my Prozac prescription. The problem was the words, you see, the terminology. It was all wrong. The Old Ones spoke a tongue a bit like Sumerian. We brought the gift of writing to humans, the power of language, the abstraction of meaning. But this vernacular English is no good... Too messy. German would be more appropriate. One of those compound words like *Todesinnenwohnenlebesfortbestand* would better express how I feel. 'Oh, eventually I'll die,' I tell her, 'but that will be tens of thousands of years in the future. Something will get me before then.'

'Garlic and crucifixes?' Angela does have a sense of humour. Apart from the Prozac it's one of the few reasons why I continue to tolerate her.

'Christ no, that's bullshit. Holy water, crucifixes, these things are useless. God is made up, at least the Christian God is. Utter nonsense. I mean, we were here long before He was invented. No, no those sorts of deterrents are harmless. You might as well try and kill me with a doughnut. I like garlic. I'm not great with bright sunlight but then I'm pale, I burn easily. Once we've been... converted or – upgraded – that would be a more up-to-date way of looking at it, we all get a little paler, we tend to prefer the night to the day, our skin gets more sensitive you know, but it's nothing some SPF 50 can't solve.'

'But you can be killed?'

'Quite easily, yes. I mean, stick a stake through my heart, cut off my head and I'll die. Not as quick as a normal human, but I'll still die. We do heal easier though, and we can survive things that would have killed us before. Here, look,' and I opened my shirt to show her a large scar across my chest. 'You see that? Took a chunk of Union shrapnel in the Civil War. It would have killed most people but my

Master looked after me. Made sure I was nourished with plentiful amounts of blood – there was a lot to go around, it was war,' I laugh, she doesn't, 'and in a couple of weeks I was right as rain. In retrospect though, the Civil War was the beginning of the end. We used to have high times I tell you, out on the plantation.'

'Previously you've described yourself as,' she would flick through her notes, 'fabulously wealthy?'

'I did all right. It's one of the virtues of living a long time. Not any more though.'

'What happened?'

'The Civil War took away my plantation. I had to change my identity, moved north. Got into finance, banking, that sort of thing. Then the crash of '29 hit me hard and since then I've never really recovered. I failed to anticipate the Second World War, didn't invest in armaments or what have you. Of course, that wiped out lots of us – there was a big flocking to join the Nazis but... anyway, the best Quarter- and Half-bloods were subtler and stayed with the Allies. Also, Jewish blood...' I turn up my nose and make a 'yuck' face. 'Anyway, it's not been great. I totally failed to grasp the whole tech bubble in the 90s, it just passed me by. I'm traditional I suppose. I invested heavily in property, got hit hard by the subprime collapse.' I shrugged, 'I guess the point is I don't have a head for business.'

'Shall we go back to the whole drinking human blood thing.'

'Hmm, okay.'

'How often do you do this?'

'Oh, I don't need to do it very often at all. I can go for years without, decades in fact. Nigger blood is best, more vital—'

'Steven, please!'

Not again. I try to change the subject. 'How old do you think I am?'

'Mid-forties?'

She's right. I look about forty-five. Not bad but sagging a bit, here and there, lines under the eyes, a dusting of grey hairs amid my thinning brown mop. 'I'm ageing rapidly,' I tell her. 'Don't you think I look older than when I saw you last week?' She writes something down, probably planning to tell me about my 'narcissistic tendencies'. I keep talking, 'I haven't... feasted for a good long time. Over two years now.' Well, since we had this conversation I've eaten a lot more. Now I look more like a guy in his mid-thirties but that's why I'm in so much trouble. 'We can go decades without eating,' I explain. 'Human blood rejuvenates us. Without it we age and get more susceptible to human illnesses, everything from a cold to cancer. Normally, these things don't bother us at all. But without blood, we get old and die. Or we have a heart attack or a stroke or you know... something gets us, eventually.'

And Angela would sigh as she scribbled ferociously in her notepad, certain, I'm sure, that my 'case' would be the one to make her career.

***

Colin drives me across the long bridge that connects Miami Beach with downtown Miami. Still mid-afternoon and the sky is a shocking blue but it feels to me as though night is almost upon us, a darkness lurking in the heart of the bright sun. Feeling a little pensive, I discreetly pop a Prozac. It all gets a bit much sometimes. We don't talk: I've told him my secret name and drunk his blood. He's shown me his cock. We're intimate enough. I continue to taste him on my lips, the metal tang of his blood. Not a vintage – I can tell he has a bad diet, too much processed food – but not bad. People tasted a lot better in the old days. They were skinnier, back then, leaner meat, but everything was organic.

We drive along a palm-lined road towards a cluster of high-rise condominiums and park in the underground basement. The elevator panel confirms the tower has fifty-five floors. Colin hits the button for the sixteenth. 'Most of these condos have been empty since the crash,' he explains, 'or they're owned by foreign investors. Either way, it's quiet here. If anyone screams, there's nobody to hear you.'

'Great.'

I want to ask what to expect but hold my tongue. What choice do I have? We stop outside a door and Colin knocks smartly, three times. The air in the corridor is cool and the white marble floors and walls smother our footsteps. I hear myself breathing.

The door opens. A Goth girl lets us in. At least, I think it's a girl, but with the short spiky hair and tubby figure it's hard to tell.

'Master,' she bows her head and kisses my hand. I wipe my fingers on my slacks.

It's a spacious apartment and would be a nice place if it didn't look like it had been decorated by two morbid fifteen-year-olds. Lots of black furnishings, horror movie posters on the walls. Why do these people think we like this shit?

'You must be tired after your travels my Master,' says the Goth girl. It's a stupid thing to say as I don't get tired or need to sleep, not in the human sense of the word anyway. She should know that. Of course, we can – if necessary – hibernate for hundreds of years. I've thought about doing it, waiting for the whole twenty-first century to just blow over but it's risky – it's very difficult to find a secure spot, somewhere safe enough to withstand whatever might happen – war, floods, ecological collapse, anything – and remote enough that no one will find me. The Old Ones are all sleeping, buried beneath the ruins of Babylon, underneath Mount Etna, the Dakota Badlands, Antarctica and many other places. It's not like I even know for sure myself. Will they ever awaken? Only in the last days and times and that might still be a long way off.

'You're safe here,' Colin adds. 'We have human blood in the fridge. You can rest, lie low and wait for things to blow over. We can put you in touch with other Quarter-bloods, that sort of thing. There's a network. We prefer LinkedIn to Facebook.'

'I see.'

'Let me take your bag.'

'Thanks.' He leaves the room with my rucksack and I take out my phone. I need to check the Web, see if there have been any new developments in my case. It was the second child that did it. That was the one that got me in trouble. The first was no bother, a dainty four-year-old 'African-American' girl I kidnapped from the mall and took out to the woods. I ripped her head off, drank her blood and hung her intestines from the trees. *It was as if little Mina had been ripped apart by a wild beast* said the horrified reporter for WSB-TV. But the second kid, only three days later, that was excessive. And stupid. A rich white girl snatched outside her high school. I forgot what my Master told me: never kill twice in the same town in the same month. And stick to the lower orders: beggars, junkies, hoboes, illegal immigrants, prostitutes, the sort of dross no one will miss. But this second kid, fuck, turns out her father was on the city council. Massive police manhunt, media blitz, potentially incriminating CCTV footage... big trouble for me. 'I don't suppose you have Wi-Fi do you?' I ask the Goth girl, who is standing at the entrance to the room watching me intently.

'Yes Master,' she bows her head, 'I'll get the code.'

I walk over to the floor-to-ceiling window. Quite a view. Over the bay clouds are gathering: white and darker blobs massing on the horizon. Perhaps this is the storm the weatherman was talking about? Once upon a time, my Master's Master could control the weather but it saddens me to think how all this knowledge has been lost.

Voices, footsteps – I turn around – there's Colin and the Goth girl and another man, a Catholic priest in a red robe, holding out a crucifix. What the—

The priest advances towards me, chanting something in Latin. It's a trap, a set-up! Fuck this. The gun – no, it's in my bag – and Colin has my bag. Fuck! The priest is chanting and waving the crucifix at me. I grab his arm and twist. He drops the crucifix and starts to scream. The red mist descends. My jaws clamp around his throat. He shudders as my fangs extend and I pull back, ripping out his thorax; blood, more crimson than his mantle, sprays everywhere. I try to snarl and look evil but Colin points something at me – a buzzing noise and I find myself on the floor, unable to move. What is this? I've been tasered. I try to get up but he zaps me again and everything dances, white and red, white and red. The Goth girl throws a net over me and despite my struggles I'm caught fast. Colin leans over, another weapon in hand, spraying me, my eyes and nose are burning and while I'm blinded a heavy chain is wrapped around the net and my arms are bound and then my legs.

'Where the fuck is the Hunter?' Colin is shouting at the Goth girl. 'Call him and let him know we've got a fresh one.'

'He texted me to say he was running late.'

'Fucking bastard killed Father O'Malley.'

I'm pulling at the chain, yanking the net, biting at it, trying to work my way free. I will slaughter these fools.

The Goth girl starts whacking me with a baseball bat. 'Stay still,' she screams, 'or I'll hit you again!' And then she hits me again, so hard it actually hurts. I stay still and it occurs to me as I lie in my chains that the death I have eluded and avoided and waited for and wept over and postponed for so long is at last upon me.

And I am so very, very frightened.

CLICKS AND HITS

I'm delayed by traffic and by the time I arrive at the Sanctuary I'm too late. What a mess! We've got us one vampire, far as I can see, bound by a net and chains, writhing and spitting like a basket full of vipers and we've got us one priest, very dead, his body covered by a blanket, his blood all over the floor. I do my best to avoid stepping in it. Colin and his girlfriend – Penny I think she's called – are standing there as if they can't quite believe what happened. Lordy lord, this won't do at all.

'Why didn't you wait for me?'

'Father O'Malley got carried away,' Colin points to the dead priest.

I'm vexed. 'What was this doo-hickey idiot even doing here?' I shout at them. 'Haven't I told you that crosses and holy water don't affect them vampires – not one little bit?'

'The Catholic Church is our main sponsor,' Colin whines at me. 'They insist we include a priest on every operation.'

I sigh and shake my head. What to do with these people? I'm tempted to kick up an almighty hullaballoo but it wouldn't do no good. Better to just focus on the 'cans' and 'shoulds' and forget about the 'should'ves' and the 'why didn't yous'. These people never learn. I walk over to the window. It's almost dark, some light wind, rain clouds bringing the dusk forward by an hour or so. Looks as if the hurricane is going to give us a miss and make landfall a few hundred miles north. Usual fuss about almost nothing. But I remember Katrina. I was there. 'I'll leave it up to you to inform the deacon about O'Malley,' I tell them. 'They will have to sort this out.' I gesture at the body. Then I turn to the vampire. 'What did you hit him with?'

'Taser, CS spray, baseball bat,' says Colin.

'Fuck you,' the vampire makes a gurgling, cussing noise. 'I will crush you like the ants that you are.' I put on some latex gloves and take a closer look. The vampire appears to be a white guy in early middle age. It snarls, showing me its teeth, long fangs gory with the priest's blood. I reach into my case and take out a syringe loaded with enough K to knock out an elephant. 'Your puny drugs won't affect me,' the vampire snarls.

I stick the needle in its bony ass. Two minutes later it's out like a baby.

***

With Colin's help, I bundle the vampire into a black body bag. It's heavier than it looks so it takes the two of us to huff and puff its body into the corridor and over to the service elevator. A cleaning lady emerges from the condo opposite but we ignore her and she ignores us. We take the elevator down to the garage basement where we heft the body into the back of my Chevy Suburban. I'm anxious to get the heck out of there as quick as I can. Now, don't get me wrong, I try not to judge folks but I've always thought there was something a bit peculiar about Colin. It's his entire method, the way he lets the vampires bite him and gets off on the whole deal. I don't approve. No, it's like I tell Carlene, I could swear these types ain't no more natural than the vampires themselves.

Anyway, I'm streaming Merle Haggard on the stereo as I head out on the old Route 41, the Tamiami Trail, just like orders say. Traffic is heavy but it falls away as soon as the swamp replaces the city, levees and drainage ditches then nothing but my lights on the road and the darkness of the Everglades. To keep my mind off it, I sing along with Merle. '*I'm lonely but I can't afford the luxury of having one I love to come along, she'd only slow me down and they'd catch up with me, for he who travels fastest goes alone.*' The song makes me feel a little lonesome so I give Carlene a call on the hands-free.

'Hello?'

'Hey babe.'

'Oh hi honey, how's it going?'

'Fairly routine I suppose. On my way to meet the boys now.'

'Did you get it?'

'Uh-huh. It killed a priest though.'

'No way? Aw, heck, that's a shame.'

'Was an awful mess.'

'Who was it?'

'O'Malley. I didn't know him.'

'Oh, well, be careful won't you honey?'

'I'm always careful sugar-pea. It's that Colin. I don't trust him. Weird little sneak.'

'How's Florida anyways?'

'Same old mess. I'll be glad to get home.'

'I miss you honey-bunny.'

'Who's my little prairie flower?'

'I am.'

'Who's my turtle dove?'

'Is it me?'

'Are you my Bambi nose?'

'I am, I am.'

'Shucks sweetheart I can't wait to squeeze you tight.'

'I don't like it when you're on the road.'

'I'll be home the day after tomorrow.'

'Be safe special cowboy.'

'I'll call in the morning okay.'

'Love you babes.'

'Love you.'

That's Carlene, my one true love. She's a good old girl. We've been sweethearts since high school. Thinking about her keeps me happy as I drive into the night, knowing that each mile I travel is one less mile between us. I go fast but then the Tamiami Trail is long and straight and runs through a whole lot of nothing and as I drive it starts to rain so I put the wipers on and then it's just me, Merle and the squeak of the wipers for nearly an hour before my satnav starts to bleep, letting me know that I'm 'approaching my destination'.

There's not much out here and what there is is easy to miss, but I see it, an old sign caught in my lights so I slow down and pull off along a dirt track. Headlights pick out a single-storey shack half sunk back into the swamp. Once upon a time it must have been a small restaurant or some sort of outlet selling Native American trinkets to passing tourists but whatever it was is long gone now.

No sign of the boys. I check my phone but there's no signal this far out. I turn the lights off and sit for a minute, listening to the rain on the windscreen. There's a banging coming from the trunk. It must be awake again.

From the glove compartment I take out a camping flashlight, the sort I can strap to my head and my .44 Magnum. It's still hot as hell, despite the rain and I walk over to the shack. No front door or anything. I wouldn't expect to find any folks out here but there's all sorts of critters might be inside so I don't take chances. Inside, no animals, just a lot of wet and rot, tendrils of plants and stuff hanging from the ceiling, pools of mud and water on the floor. Clouds of mosquitos. My flashlight picks out droppings and such but nothing of concern.

Satisfied, I go back to the Chevy and put on a white plastic forensic suit. Lordy lord I do declare I've been eating so much of Carlene's fried chicken I can't hardly squeeze it over my gut. It ain't so comfortable, wearing the suit over my regular clothes what with the humidity and all but I don't want to mess myself up. I hear the sound of an approaching vehicle and pause – is it them? No, they keep going, whoever they are.

Well well well. Anyways, I'm used to this. This is what I do. I might be from New Orleans but my great, great grandfather was from Romania. We're part of a long tradition and it's like I says to my Carlene, 'duty is duty'. Better this than that anyhow. Time for a cigarette and more Merle.

I sit back in the Chevy, having a smoke and singing along. It keeps kicking and shouting in the back so I turn the music up some more. The boys still ain't here and although it would be easier if they were it don't make all that much difference. I'd rather be gone sooner than later so I figure I might just as well make a start. Wish we could have met somewhere more convenient but they have their reasons and I understand. I get out again, open the trunk, grab the vampire and roll it out. It hits the floor with a wallop and starts to swear.

'You cut that out now,' I says as I drag it writhing and thrashing about in the bag into the ruined shack. Phew. I go back to the Chevy and take out an axe, a bowie knife and an ice cooler.

I unzip the body bag and pull it away from the vampire. It's still tight bound by the chains but has bitten through the net. In the torchlight I see its face, twisted with hatred and spite. It hisses, its jaw distending, fangs protruding, trying to wriggle away, biting and snapping at the air. I have another smoke and watch it for a bit. 'Funny, you know,' I says, 'but we've been doing this for many a generation, you and I.'

'I've got money,' it snarls. 'I can make you rich. However much they're paying you—'

'—Oh, it ain't 'bout the money son. My great, great grand-pappy was from Transylvania. He put a stake through your great, great grand-pappy's black heart.'

'You don't know what you're talking about, insect!'

'Oh, but that's where you're wrong. Well wrong. Your reign of terror has come to an end.' With a sigh, I pick up the axe with my right hand, put one boot atop its head and bring the axe down. It takes three goes. There's always a lot less blood in a vampire than you might imagine. The head rolls off into the darkness. It's still making a racket, hissing and cussing me out but that's all right. Vampires don't die quite like decent folk. I wait for its arms and legs to stop thrashing then I pull the chains and the net off the body and put them with the body bag. I'm about to start cutting with the bowie knife when I hear a vehicle arrive, headlights illuminating the room. I go outside, keeping one hand close to my .44. You can't be too careful.

Well well well. I thought so. It's the boys. I recognise their black Lincoln Navigator. 'Y'all is late,' I say.

'Good to see you bro,' says the first. Mr Bradley, I think it is. Mr Bradley and Mr Smith. I struggle to tell them apart in their black suits.

'It's in here.'

'Done?'

'Almost.'

They follow me into the ruin. Smith (or is it Bradley?) takes one look at the headless body and goes back outside again. The darn softie. The other steps back while I get to work. I make a cut just below its collarbone and slice down to the navel. As I said, there's less blood than you'd expect in a vampire, but a nasty smell emerges, not a natural smell, if you know what I mean, but the sort of stench that sticks to the back of your throat. Makes you want to choke. Good Lord. I've got it open up now, guts and everything. This is why I wear the suit. Smith (or is it Bradley) is less squeamish, leaning in trying to see as my head-lamp lights the insides of the vampire.

'That it?'

'Yessir.'

Where you and I might have a heart and lungs, the vampire has... this. It looks a bit like a jellyfish, oozing around the internal organs. Green and pulsing, little tendrils and polyps attached to ribs and what have you. Something a bit like a red light seems to glow within it and I have the sense, as I always do at this stage, that it's watching me. Two quick cuts and I can pull it out. It writhes and flexes in my hands.

'The cold box, quick.'

Smith (or Bradley) passes me the box and I drop it in.

'There you are.'

I shut the box. This is what the boys want. Carlene and I often speculate about who they are. We have three theories: agents of the Illuminati, agents of Opus Dei or CIA agents. Maybe it's all the same, who knows for sure? They claim to be 'Homeland Security' whatever that means. We often wonder what they do with the vampire hearts. Analyse them, I guess, look for uses, medical or military. Shucks. It's not for me to know. I trust my government but I ain't dumb. Bradley (or Smith) hands me a sack full of cash. Fifty thousand bucks. Not bad for a night's work.

'Don't forget, you have to feed it,' I add. 'One rodent or something similar every twelve hours.'

They leave. I put the net, the chains and the body bag into the back of the Chevy. I'm fair pissing sweat, if you'll excuse my French. I pick up the severed head and toss it into the shack. Then I go back into the shack with a can of gasoline and slosh it about. Add a match and get out fast. I doubt the fire will be enough to destroy everything, but it helps cover up the traces. Finally, I take off the forensic suit and gloves, adding them to the other equipment. I'll dispose of all these later. That's better. I notice it has stopped raining. There's no sign of the fire out here but I smell smoke. I get back into the Chevy and turn onto the main road. I drive for a minute or two before putting the headlights on and keep going; Waylon, Kris, Johnny and friends keep me company.

***

Around two a.m. I check into a Motel 6 on the outskirts of Naples. I'm bushed but it's hard to wind down after everything I've done. I keep my .44 by the bed and log on with my laptop. I browse *YouthTube* for a bit, catching up with some of my favourites, Tiffany and Corine but best of all is Kimberly. She's such a sweet, down home girl. There's a video she made singing a Shelby Lynn number while sitting in a fifties diner drinking a pink milkshake that I do adore. Of course, there's a lot of bad stuff on *YouthTube*, a side bar of temptation with all those nasty black and red vids, flashing banners advertising all sorts like the latest Trixxxie Foxxx gangbang video for just $5.99 but I do my best to ignore them. Afterwards, I say my prayers. I know God ain't no direct use when it comes to dealing with a vampire but that's cause they ain't exactly what we might call supernatural creatures and I'm safe in bed which is all that matters at the end of the day, so I'm thankful. Them vampires is monsters, that's all.

I'd like to say I sleep well, but I don't.

***

Two days later I'm in Mobile trying to chase a few leads. I'm searching for one Lester Newman, a car thief who recently jumped bail. That's my main profession, a bounty hunter. I bring fugitives to justice. The vampire slaying, that's more a side line, a lucrative one at that, even if it be deep in my family tradition. Anyhow, vampires or felons, I don't see much of a difference, just different sides of the same flipped coin.

I spend the afternoon driving around a few areas where Newman is known to have associates and family members. I try knocking on some doors but the doors stay closed. The sky is grey even if it's still fiercely hot and Mobile is even more quiet than I might have said was normal. There's scarce a soul on the streets, just them flat, low buildings, wrought iron shacks and the heat, radiating off the sidewalk. I spend some time in the sort of neighbourhood you don't want to spend no time in at all, not when you're a white man doing the job I do. Low wooden houses half swallowed up by the Alabama green with big yards and peeling porches and railings over the doors and windows. A car slows down and some brothers take a long hard look at me and I'm thankful for the .44. After a while I head back to the hotel.

I could call it quits and push on home but I decide to spend another night in Mobile. I don't give up so easily. That evening, I go to a bar downtown that Lester was known to frequent. It's a long shot, if I'm honest, so I'm not expecting anything but I take a stool by the bar and order a tomato juice and show the barmaid his photo. She just turns up her nose and says, 'Never seen him.' She looks like a nice gal, despite the tats all over her arms.

The bar ain't so bad. I'm comfortable enough on my stool observing the scene. The lighting is low and there seems to be a bunch of regulars. A young guy sits next to me. I notice the barmaid leaves the bottle of Jack beside his glass. He shoots and swallows. There's a couple of good ol' boys getting drunk in a booth and making a racket like their pay just came in but mostly it's men on their own and most heads are turned to the TV on the wall above the bar. It's tuned to *YouthTube Live!* and as it's past nine they're plugging the black and red vids real hard. There's that Trixxxie Foxxx again, her eyes smeared with shadow and wearing a blue wig. 'Hey fellas!' she wiggles her pierced tongue at the bar. 'Check out my channel, TubeTrixxxie where I'll be live-streaming something special for y'all later.' My, my, my, now I don't have eyes for no woman except my Carlene but I must say, that Trixxxie, she certainly is quite the looker, if you follow.

The old boys in the booth get real excited by the sight of her and start hollering and carrying on. I gather Trixxxie was a local girl once upon a time. She must live in Los Angeles with the rest of them now. 'I'd give that bitch somethin',' one of the old boys calls out, 'I'd rip her open wide.' I glance at the barmaid to see if any of this profanity is bothering her but she's texting on her phone, not bothered at all far as I can tell.

The young man next to me though, he seems bothered. He knocks back two or three shots of Jack in a row, real hard and desperado like. I take another look at the ol' boys, trying to work out how much trouble they'd be. I figure they wouldn't be no trouble at all. I ain't a young man and Lord knows I ain't fit like I used to be but I can handle myself, if you follow. Not that I go looking for a fight. A strong man knows how to avoid violence, that's what I always say. I admit, I've shot down a few men in my time, but none that didn't deserve it.

'Fucking assholes,' the young man mutters to himself.

'You all right there son? You want to go easy with that.'

The guy is startled and faces me with drunk, angry eyes. I can tell he didn't expect no one to speak to him.

'No offence meant partner,' I'm looking to cool him down. 'Just that when you're drinking alone like that, you got to be careful. I speak from experience. Me, I used to have a bad relationship with the bottle. Now,' I point to my glass, 'tomato juice.' I'll have to tell you about my drinking days some other time. If it weren't for Carlene, I'd be dead drunk in a ditch right now. 'If it weren't for my good wife—' I begin.

'Trixxxie Foxxx tonight!' the TV announcer cuts me off. There's a montage of the girl clad in various peculiar outfits. The men start hollering again.

'Are those boys bothering you?' I ask the young man. I can see he's distressed. 'I don't appreciate their profanity much either, 'specially not when there's a lady present.' I nod at the barmaid who is still on her phone.

The young man appears confused. He has long hair and brushes it from his face. 'Those men?' he says.

'The boys there. That's right. I can have a word, tell them to keep it down.'

He screws his face up and for a minute I think he's going to cuss me but then he leans in. 'Guess what?' he says, reeking of liquor. 'I know that girl.'

'Her?' I nod at the barmaid.

'No. Her.' He points at the television. 'Trixxxie.'

'Well now...' I think the young man must be joking but then I see he's not. 'You're serious?'

'You fucking bet your fucking life I'm serious.' His hands are shaking as he pours himself another shot.

The boy is hurting bad and the way I see it, when you're hurting like that it's good to tell someone about it. These are lonesome times. 'Allow me to introduce myself. My name is Abraham Helsing. Pleased to make your acquaintance.' He grunts and nods. 'You seem to me like you're burdened with something son. We all get like that. You can tell me about it, if you want.'

'You? Why should I tell you anything?'

'No reason son. You look burdened, that's all. I'll carry a little of that burden, if you like.'

'You wouldn't understand.'

'Perhaps not, but I've been around. Heck, I've seen things would turn your hair white.'

The young man scrutinises me a long minute, as if he's weighing up the situation and can't decide if he wants to talk or just drink. Well, I know that feeling.

'Okay,' he says at last. 'Yeah. I guess. Fuck it. Why not?'

'I'm all ears.' I gesture at the barmaid to give me another tomato juice.

The kid takes a deep breath. 'Her real name is Madison. Madison Parker Lee.'

'That's a nice name,' I say.

'We were at college together. She was just... I don't know. A nice ordinary kinda girl, you know.'

'You were sweethearts?'

'That's right.' He wipes a little sweat from his lips. 'Sweethearts. She liked sex though. She was... highly sexed...' The word lingers between us. 'You can tell, can't you?' he gestures at the screen again although they've switched from showing Trixxxie to some half-naked black boy juggling bottles.

'Oh, I wouldn't know.' I'm glad it's dark in the bar so the boy can't see me blush.

'Hey, you don't need to pretend. She gets twenty million hits a day. A day! Sometimes more. I don't think there's a man in the world with a Wi-Fi connection who hasn't jerked off to one of her videos.'

'Well if there is you're looking at him. I don't appreciate none of that.'

He stares at me in astonishment, like I just told him I could walk through fire. 'You telling me you ain't never seen one of her videos? Bullshit. You serious?'

'Sure am.'

'Jesus tells you not to, is that it?'

'I don't think Jesus would approve but I don't... Shucks, call me old fashioned if you like but my wife, Carlene, she's enough for me. Anyway, all that stuff...' I shake my head. 'I guess it ain't to my taste.' It's true. I don't appreciate these things at all. I have a sudden urge to show the boy the photo I got of Carlene in my wallet but he won't think nothing of it. She don't look much like Trixxxie.

The boy smiles a dark sort of smile, like he knows I won't like what he has to say but knows he has to say it anyway. 'If that's true perhaps you really are the person to talk to.'

I sip my juice. 'Could be.'

He takes a deep breath. 'We'd been dating for a couple of years, going steady, when I had the idea... And, well, she was going to go away for a few weeks, so while we was doing it one night I hit on the notion of taking some photos of us, just with my phone. I said it would be something for me to look at while she was gone, said I'd rather look at pictures of her than some other girl on the Internet or in a magazine. Funny thing was I thought she'd be like no way but...' he rests his hand on his glass, contemplating another shot. 'She got into it, you know? She liked it. The camera turned her on. It was almost like... shit, I guess it was like I'd awoken something inside her.'

'I suppose some girls are like that,' I say. It ain't a subject I could ever imagine raising with Carlene, but we can't pretend there isn't a whole lot of craziness out there.

'She looked good in the pictures.'

'I'm sure she did. She's a fine looking young lady.'

His eyes glaze over and he hesitates. 'So, she went away for three weeks and while she was gone I put some of them up on this site. A website for amateurs, girlfriends, DIY shit you know, that sorta stuff. *Myexgirlfriend.com* it was called.'

'Why would you do a thing like that?'

'I don't know. I guess I liked the idea. I thought it was kinky. I thought it might turn me on, imagining all the other people looking at the photos.'

'You didn't think she'd mind?'

'I did, but I figured... fuck, I suppose I said to myself that she would never know. I could always claim my phone got hacked or something.' He takes another drink. 'In truth I don't understand why I did it. I just did. I put them on and when I looked back, a few days later, I see these pics have been viewed like thousands of times. I mean thousands.

Hundreds of comments. People fucking love these photos. Or they love her. No one really gives a shit about me. I'm just the cock, I realise. They don't even *notice* me. It's the girl they want to see.'

'Uh-huh.'

'And, well, so I get thinking. I mean, money ain't so good, I ain't got none and Madison ain't really got none either so when she gets back I tell her my idea. I show her what I done and tell her my idea.'

'Right.'

'At first she's mad, you know, like what the fuck? But then she calms down and I see... it's like she gets the idea too. But bigger. Or brighter. So we make more pics. We set up a tripod for the phone and video ourselves doing it. Normal shit. Kinky shit, all sorts. We make like five or six little movies and put them on the site. I didn't realise at the time, but *YouthTube* own that site.'

'Well I'll be.'

'It's all about the hits, you see. Clicks and hits. On them sites you can make some money, if you get enough. It's not a lot, it's like a hundred bucks or so per ten thousand views but I figure, hell, why not? Madison is into it. It's fun, we like fucking, we look good fucking and who cares? And we're getting so many clicks that in the first month we get three thousand dollars. Three thousand! That's more than we were making doing anything else.'

I take a sip of juice. The old boys have calmed down some.

'We'd been doing it for about six months. The last couple of months we'd pulled in thirty thousand, something like that. Man, I was on cloud nine. I thought this is it, me and Madison gonna make good money together doing what we do anyway. That's when the call came.' He wipes at his face. There's a faint shake to his voice. 'To Madison. They wanted to speak to Madison. Not me. Some folks in Los Angeles. Called themselves *YouthTube Elite*. Said they had a contract for three million dollars. Said Madison was a 'natural born pornstar'. Said they'd make Madison the hottest star on the channel. Madison. Not me.'

'That a fact.'

'I was just the cock. I didn't matter. So she signed the contract and off she went. What we did was over. When I tried to stop her she told me I was holding her back, stopping her from "empowering herself". We hadn't really thought much about the business part, with our little thing. I didn't think we needed to. She was getting fifty per cent, even-stevens but they was offering a whole lot more. Madison died that day and three weeks later,' he nods at the screen, 'Trixxxie Foxxx was born.' He takes another drink. I have a sip of juice, just to go along with the kid. He's got my stomach all knotted up. 'And now... well, I'm never more than two clicks away from watching her get fucked every which way by God knows who, see her do all sorts of things I could never even imagine...' His voice shakes and for a moment the poor kid looks like he's going to cry. 'Biggest goddam pornstar on the planet. Goddam. I did that. Me. I did it.'

Ah hell. I put a hand on his shoulders. 'You loved her, didn't you?'

'Yeah,' he wipes at his eyes, 'I guess I did.'

***

Although it's late I don't feel tired anymore so I check out of the hotel, drink a cup of Joe and hit the road. Only a hundred and fifty miles to home and I'm streaming the Dixie Chicks greatest hits over the radio. Times like this I'm sure grateful I got my Carlene.

YOU'VE GONE TOO FAR THIS TIME

I/she/Trixxxie opened my/her mouth to the fourteenth and fifteenth cocks after the blur of gyration-penetration the thrashing smashing the two cocks groaning their cum joining that of cocks one through thirteen in hot splashes over my/her face as I/she take both in my/her mouth to slush to gurgle in a yum yum yum, a frothy white churn, a cock-a-chino until the director shouts 'cut' and the men fade to shower, smoke, eat a burger leaving their seed a slimy baptism over I/she/Trixxxie/me, my/her/our ass/pussy aching throbbing front to back from the many penetrations so much so I/she/Trixxxie can hardly stand on wobbly legs oh dear well fuck it look how they look at her, at me with fear with reverence with disgust with awe because I/she/Trixxxie is everything they want, everything they hate and I/she/Trixxxie is radiant with that and I/she/Trixxxie am/is not they. The shower is hot and strong the water washes it away but not the ache not the event not the action does it matter? Christ this gang-bang took it out of us.

I/she/Trixxxie is in the car glazed and spaced Los Angeles hazy HOLLYWOOD written faint in the hills on the phone checking *YouthTube* the video up 175,000 hits already just an hour old hit refresh 176,000 hits hit refresh, I/she refresh myself/Trixxxie I if only. I/she/Trixxxie the digital bitch avatar these cocks, this pussy can never die, hardest working cunt in the west. Home, Xanax, vodka and ice refresh Twitter five thousand new followers this week links to the video twenty thousand retweets I/she/Trixxxie bank balance flush as the new video drops fifteen men on I on she Trixxxie Foxxx and a tidal wave of cum their red faces groaning and yearning but I/she/Trixxxie can take it take it take it and more. This is nothing.

***

I/she/Trixxxie interviewed for *LA Weekly*. 'I disagree that what I do demeans women, yes I'm aware of what she said about me,' talking talking talking, 'but she doesn't know shit she wants to hold women back, she wants to say what women can or can't be what we should or shouldn't do, we need to redefine feminism, I mean what is more feminist than using what you've got to get what you want right? Does she get a million hits? She does not and anyway I don't let any man own my body, I'll share it with all but none can own me egalitarian I am, yes that's right because I'm truly free do you know what freedom means? Most people, most women are too scared to be free, they worry too much what others think about them they hate me because they don't like to see a woman who isn't afraid because I'm not afraid I do what I want exactly what I want to do, I do, sex is work, fucking is work, sucking cocks is work, so why not get paid? Something tangible, something that means something you know? Not love, I'm talking digits in the bank, I'm talking clicks and hits. If you're going to fuck a man you should get paid for it, that's what I say. I know lots of feminists they love me even the haters they think of me when they jerk off, when they cum they think of me it's the wives I feel most sorry for letting their men define who they are what they should do, well not me no. *YouthTube* needs me they don't own me, I'm Trixxxie Foxxx no one owns me. It's not abuse it's freedom, I'll fuck for a million dollars, I'll fuck for none. No don't let children watch my videos, that's the fault of the parents you know I'll bet there isn't a father in the land not one doesn't watch me on the sly when his wife is out when his kids are in bed, the Christians are the worst fuck them and don't blame me for that that's men they've always been like that.' Sweet intense girl with goofy glasses and a big smile squirming as I/she/Trixxxie tells it like it is. 'Do I make you wet honey? I bet you've never had a girl look at you this way before have you. Does your boyfriend make you cum? Oh you don't have one? Oh but you're so cute come here let Trixxxie tell you, show you something, you'll thank me you will I know it.'

***

My/her sister calls, and says, 'Madison you've gone too far this time,' then, 'they're praying for you in church these last few nights.' The priest calls me the crimson harlot, the whore of Babylon, says my videos are the work of Satan, says the mark of Satan is on my brow, says that when I spread my legs I hasten the end of the world and I tell her I remember that same priest he tried to touch me once when I was fifteen still a girl but with this womanly body he couldn't take his eyes off my tits even as he was talking about sin and temptation and damnation he was fucking me with his eyes he's no different I tell her he's just another sweaty dirty man hiding in the shadows. My/her sister says think about Daddy, our daddy's ill he can't take it anymore, he says you've broken his heart and Momma's even worse she won't stop she's at the church all day and all night praying for your soul and I say oh right how much money does she want? I bought her a house. Does she want a chateau in the south of France? Does she want ten thousand fifty thousand what does she want? Fuck it, I tell my sister I'll pay it don't matter anything to get her off my back. She says did you hear about Brandon I/she/we're like who? She says don't pretend you don't remember, Brandon, your boyfriend did you hear? And I/she try to remember but there have been so many cocks they're all just cocks not boyfriends, but Madison she says he got into a fight with some fellas at a bar they smashed his head in he's in hospital he's in a bad way he was asking after you think about what you did to that poor boy. I/we say did what? Poor boy what? He's no poor boy there's no poor boys he did it to himself, he did all this to himself it was his idea anyway, I don't remember and she says you've changed. We've all changed I/we tell her change is what happens, don't blackmail me with your bullshit and as we talk I/we refresh my phone. Five million views in 48 hours. Trixxxie/I/we/she/me.

***

Trixxxie's agent is on the line, and he says sweetheart here's the deal and you've got to go with me on this one, there's a party in the desert, Palm Springs all the bosses will be there, President Buer will be there, he wants to thank you personally you're the guest of honour it's time to think big, this is just the start we're going to make so much fucking $$$ and the car comes at three. I/she/Trixxxie says I'm so tired that last one took it out of me I'm hurting my pussy needs rest is it absolutely necessary? He says, babe it's the most important event of the year you'll be there it's an order but I/we say no man gives Trixxxie orders, but he says honey this ain't no man calling the shots you won't regret it trust me there's more riding on this than you might think and we're the ones, he says, we'll be the ones who decide what is or what is not the car will come at three you better be ready. I/she says Trixxxie's always fucking ready ready ready the car the car the car the desert the desert the desert flashes by on the highway, I/she/we Trixxxie Foxxx in the back watching the sky blue and limitless through tinted windows through dark sunglasses flicking through Twitter the lovers and the haters I hope you die you sick fucking bitch they tweet. I/we favourite all the trolls give them a little taste of the love they need I/we look there's a cactus there's a distant mountain there's a gas station a Taco Bell, all these places I/we have been and have not been, just an Alabama girl at heart sweet home Alabama all that cracker shit that my daddy listens to, no Trixxxie Foxxx is beyond that and what did the agent say? They will all be there, all the *YouthTube* bosses, a gathering the desert in Palm Springs what's Palm Springs like I/ she thinks? Golf courses in the desert old rich people old men with suntans and speedos by the pool smiling with gold chains I/she thinks this but where did the image come from? It went like this on her knees sucking cocks one through to four alternately cocks five to fifteen background stroking lurking some taste salty others of nothing only perhaps just the spermy testosterone drip drip of men-ness tasting it all the time no matter what we eat now cocks two and three alternating fucking her behind as I/she/Trixxxie sucks cocks one and four with cocks five and six in either hand the camera woman with the Gopro zooming in then something then something cocks nine and ten taking turns fucking I/we/Trixxxie lying on our back other cocks zooming in and out of her/ my/our open lips and hands I/she/we thinks then sitting on one cock reverse cowgirl they call it in the trade others rotating a clock of cocks a twelve thirteen fourteen hands on our waist hands on our butt lifting us/we/Trixxxie up and down mouths and then hands on our breasts bending us/we/Trixxxie over cock ten in our ass then cock twelve then cock four now on we back cock four in ass cocks two, seven, nine, eleven in pussy one after the other alternating with lips, the cocks, the men red faced groaning—

I/she/we refreshes our phone. Trixxxie/I/we/she/me. Eight million views in sixty hours.

***

On the outskirts I/she/Trixxxie think we must be on the outskirts the sun is setting the sky a luminous a beautiful pink pink yes turning off the highway along a straight empty road lined with palm trees with distant mountains it's flat, this place and everything is low as if scared to rise above one storey. Gates open there are torches and the car stops in front of a modern bungalow type building. What is it? A house a gallery a museum a hotel an office? I/she feels a sudden nostalgia for the gentle streets of Mobile, the gracious mansions with white balconies and pillars where I/she imagined we might live one day like a proper Southern belle, sitting out on the porch in the evening sun receiving gentleman callers but the sentiment doesn't last long as a man in a smart suit with an earpiece opens the car door and bows slightly as I/she/Trixxxie emerges into the hot desert and walks forward. There are torches flickering and a strong Wi-Fi signal. Through the house glass rooms fold out to a courtyard open to the stars a patio and an enormous pool and tall palm trees in enormous pots and look I/she/Trixxxie recognise many people and everybody recognises me. Where's my/her/Trixxie's agent Balam he said he'd be here? Where is he? I/she should call him, oh hello, hello, hello. There are people frolicking in the pool but more just circulating all dolled up in their finest very genteel like. There's Tesanna, there's Billy-Boy, hello hello, there's Sara DuPoc who made black and reds and then transitioned to the mega-mainstream with that song 'Peek-A-Boo' no one can forget. Many black and reds got more hits and clicks than the mega-mainstreamers but that isn't the point. Sara pretends not to see her/me/Trixxxie fuck the haters I/she/we take a glass of champagne take an olive some guy says hi and simpers about meeting me and I/she move away with a gracious nod Trixxxie has no time for this and there's a hand on my arm it's Balam he's here after all, honey he says, Trixxxie darling and touches my arm he has a new ring I notice the head of a hawk on his finger its beautiful shiny and he says let me introduce you and I forget their names, *YouthTube* people middle-aged men ordinary looking men but with good hair good teeth and real friendly 'we're big fans of your work' they say I bet you are horny-boy and they talk about sponsorship with Nascar and a tie-in with a phone app and I/she/we/ Trixxxie say bring it baby. Balam says he'll work out the details have more champagne darling have more of these what are these? Quail eggs honey what do you think? I'm good at putting balls in my mouth I/we say he laughs. Way to go.

***

Another long low modern bungalow out back surrounded by cactuses and a lawn with a sprinkler going *pfff pfff pfff* a hint of moisture in the air and the path is lit by candles in pots. President Buer he says. I/we think this might be a big deal but glad we dressed appropriately a white vintage McQueen dress and heels a classy thing not a black-and-red thing, when I/she/we show it all in our work we cover it for play that's the way you do it. Everyone here seen my/her/Trixxxie spread pussy gaping asshole seen it all so cover up cover up that was good advice, first good advice we got when we came to this town this business. Inside, air conditioning is strong and a large room with glass windows to the floor on one side but it's dark out, no desert view. Balam behind I/she/me is he nervous? I smell something that man-funk he reeks of it then I/ we hear things and the lights come on there are three men standing there naked cocks half-erect. What is this I/ she/Trixxxie turns and says to Balam – there's a camera woman too – you never said we was doing a shoot and he says go with the flow honey don't worry you'll be paid you'll be more than paid what does more than paid fucking mean? but then a fourth man is there, behind the rest, this man is huge he must be twice as tall as the others must be fifteen feet tall he's huge he's wearing a long black robe of silk but his arms are bare and tanned copper brown and rippling with muscles he's a giant he's incredible his face handsome and rugged like a mountain top, he has brown eyes and a long straight beard like the beard of an ancient king and a huge bow and arrows over his shoulder as if he must have been hunting a beast even more giant than he and we/she/I fucking hell and he says congratulations Trixxxie I am President Buer I help to create *YouthTube* you are one of our brightest and biggest stars and as he speaks it's like there's a contraction and I/we see he's not so tall maybe six seven six eight but not a giant but he's there and the cocks are being stroked and he says I want to see you in action for myself with a nice smile and his voice is gentle I imagine him in meetings and negotiations, talking and winning, talking and winning. You'll get 100% of the advertising revenue for this one, just for this one. You'll do that? Sure Trixxxie Foxx will do that this guy he's a cock another cock I'll even do him too if he wants I look at my agent he's sweating and he nods. No rest for this wicked we think.

***

I/she/we remember when we arrived in Los Angeles, nervous first timer nervous virgin-like pussy fuck and she/we said to me/myself this is what we must be no more Madison bury her give birth to Trixxxie Foxxx that's a great name Balam said, there was a girl, Fontana May, biggest star before I/me/we she said sweetheart split yourself to do this job, it is and it isn't you it's more than you, become the other you always were become it so I/we did we did we did but sometimes she/I/Madison would dream of a white statue recovered from the ocean, statue of a man with a high crown the stone washed smooth by the water, refresh six million clicks and hits, refresh and the statue lay on the beach on the shore in the black sand and she saw a centaur hunting stags with bow and arrow HOLLYWOOD faded sign faint in the haze on the horizon there must be no more Madison, erase it all it never happened life started when the aeroplane landed at LAX nothing before, a nothing like the desert, a nothing like the bungalow in the desert the silhouette of a palm tree burning against the pussy pink sky. Fontana said we can live forever you know there is a place in Dakota buried deep in the earth all the secrets are there, pour the vials you must pour the vials. They will suck the secrets from the earth she says I've seen you work you have it too and she smiled: she had a lovely smile Fontana May, a smile that seemed to draw you/me/we from her face to her breasts and butt oh the endless sweet dream of a womanly body, the million-dollar dream said Balam, you're not a pornstar they never called it that they called her a dream-maker LOL. There is a kiss says Fontana May that is sweeter than all the rest, a very special kiss a kiss that opens your eyes forever that is like an endless sigh into golden light like honey you know it's like being cast back back back to when you were happiest when were you happiest there must have been such a time (yes I/she/Madison remembering the lake where we went for summer holidays when we were a little girl but it wasn't even the lake wasn't even the holiday it was the drive we remembered because we had never travelled so everything was new mysterious beautiful whereas now it's all flat flat flat unreal) and she went on like that you know honey she said once upon a time giants walked the Earth ruled the Earth it's in the Bible or is it one of the other books one of the ones they left out. Oh I don't go for that had enough of that growing up this is a sin, that's a sin guess my soul is damned to hell but Fontana just smiled and said they made the pyramids, Stonehenge all these other places in Turkey, Iraq, Syria, Peru they were made by giants half men half angels didn't you always want to be an angel well I don't know but they made a vid together anyway Fontana May versus Trixxxie Foxxx versus two cocks sucking fucking cock to ass cock to mouth dp for her dp for she/me licking that pussy kissing those tits cum swapping refresh ten million views and counting. And it came to pass she read later in the hotel they were in a hotel for this one that when the children of men had multiplied she read that in those days were born unto them beautiful and comely daughters and the angels and she read that the children of heaven saw and lusted after them, the angels and the beautiful cummy daughters and they said to one another, 'Come, let us choose us wives from among the children of men and beget us children' and they were men and women the angels liquid bodies, bodies of light, golden cocks and fragrant vibrating vaginas and there was nothing forbidden nothing that could not be done or was not done I/she thought of that time when Balam took me/her/ Trixxxie to another party in Beverly Hills another house made of glass flat and open and there were naked men everywhere tanned handsome men with six packs perfect pecs steroid strong bodies some of them sleeping some of them stood still as statues and we sat by the pool the water was cold the sun was hot and in one corner some of the men were fucking a girl was it even being filmed or was it just one of those things? A man held our hand and said sometimes out here you can hear the wolves at night, sometimes they come down from the hills and rummage through the garbage wolves yes wolves and wild cats as well we are all the children of Cain he said gently touching our hand, he was an old man but sort of ageless they get like that in LA his face hardly moving with Botox and whatnot but no scars. I know a very good plastic surgeon people would tell her but Balam said no he said keep your tits natural doesn't matter if they're a little small natural is better anyone can have big fake tits don't fuck with your USP you're like the girl next door but the girl next door who is so hot the whole neighborhood goes mad to get a piece of that ass. And the old man he said you're new here shall I show you my sleeping boys sleeping staying beautiful waiting for the seventh trumpet to blow and the great Tribulation to shake the dead from their graves to shake the righteous to heaven to waken the sleepers and the watchers and you could live forever—

***

Next morning we sat in the car taking us back to LA and we felt good. We had scratched our neck sometime in the night, two small marks and they itched like love bites. We remembered Buer took our hand took us to one side to a private room his hand huge like it could crush our skull but he was tender, he was kind his words were soft, his dark eyes filled with a feeling we could feel all over us but not quite comprehend: a tenderness and a sadness and it was like we are not sure what it was like, was it like the universe was it like the ocean was it like the distant mountains we saw from the car was it like the desert that starts just the other side of the wall? There is a kiss said Fontana there is a kiss said Buer. Perhaps it was the dream, scratched ourselves in the dream we thought, the scratch the mark on our neck but it wasn't a dream it was a nightmare really more like a nightmare, we ripping them apart, the hunky-fuck-cocks, tearing off their flesh and peeling their skin and reaching into their stomach to unravel intestines purple and long, lungs and heart, bathing in their blood not cocks this time but flesh in our mouth chewing and swallowing yum yum tasted so good... and we didn't wake up, we didn't wake up feeling disgusted we woke up hungry and empty and so hungry like nothing like no food would ease this hunger and we could see it feel it in the people around us the red essence pumping through them the vitality, the life force all the desire that can never be fulfilled. We sat in the car trying to remember if we had in fact slept although we did not feel tired we felt very awake and our ass didn't burn anymore and our pussy didn't hurt anymore no we felt strong we felt good we felt like we could fuck a thousand cocks or more what did it matter? We check our phone the most recent video already up 450,000 views and counting

I WANT TO GO AND LIVE IN NORWAY

As I expected, we don't get nearly as far as Mom said we would. Last night we slept in some parking lot and it was like a zombie horror show when this homeless freak banged on the car windows at four a.m. I wasn't asleep – how can anyone sleep in a car parked up next to an abandoned grocery store on the outskirts of a strange town? Mom can, I guess, but she jumped awake as the homeless guy mashed his face against the window. She screamed, started the car and we drove off leaving the zombie waving at our taillights.

Back on the Interstate Mom tried to act as if what had happened was a normal thing, 'Early starts are good dontcha think Esther?' But come two in the afternoon and she's flagging, mumbling prayers and such under her breath and I'm also exhausted but I don't dare to close my eyes for fear she might zzz off at the wheel. All day her phone has been buzzing with texts – I don't know if they are from Dad or the other guy, Earl – but obviously it's down to me to suggest we stop. We pass a sign for a town called Rome and Mom decides it's an 'omen', but it must have been a bad one as the town is some distance from the Interstate and when we finally find it Rome is nothing to write home about. I'm not sure what Mom was expecting, like maybe she'd get a glimpse of the Pope and the Whore of Babylon riding in a jewelled chariot together down Main Street, but she settles for an Economy Inn on the road back out of town. Four in the afternoon and we're still in Georgia.

'North Dakota is two thousand miles away,' I say as Mom parks the car. Her phone buzzes again and she ignores me to focus on sending a reply. I want to ask her who keeps texting but I know she'll just tell me to 'mind my own business' so I do that.

It's hot, just as hot as back in Florida. I don't like the room which is small and dingy with a musty smell but is much better than spending another night in the car. We go inside and Mom takes her bottle of vodka from her handbag and a plastic cup from the bathroom. 'Be a doll and go tell the man at reception we'll take it. Oh, and get us some ice.'

I don't like it when she calls me 'a doll' but I go and get ice from the machine at reception anyway. The only trace of the receptionist is a sign saying, 'Back in five minutes'. The doors to the rooms opposite ours are open and I see kids and women wandering randomly from one to the other while two very fat men are slumped on fold-out chairs drinking beer. They all seem to know each other. A boy about my age or maybe a bit older walks past with his shirt off. I watch him a while and wonder what he's doing here.

Back in the room and Mom has pulled the curtains shut and turned the A/C on full blast. She's lying on the bed wearing just bra and sweatpants, smoking a cigarette and scrolling through her phone. I notice she's got Dad's old .45 on the bedside table but decide it's best not to mention it. Mom's a lousy shot. 'Bring it here,' she orders, scooping several cubes from the bucket without even so much as a thank you. The TV is on, that show again, *Cop Cam*. We seem to be in a cop car, a dash-mounted camera giving a view of the road. 'THERE'S THE SUSPECT' says a voice and the car accelerates straight towards this African-American man strolling along minding his business. His back is to us so he doesn't even see the car when it rams into him. There's a brief flash of his surprised face as he flies over the hood. Then we see the cops cuffing him as he lies on the ground screaming. Now they cut back to the studio where the presenter, a fat middle-aged man who used to be a sheriff in Texas and still dresses like it, knocks back his head and laughs uproariously. Mom laughs too. 'Well the perpetrator weren't badly injured and he was wanted for fifteen outstanding speeding tickets. Fifteen! And he was a known marijuana user. *Cop Cam* justice folks,' and he whacks his nightstick against the fake desk in his fake office. 'Officers shot themselves dead six perpetrators this week, including a kidnapper, a meth dealer, a notorious jaywalker and an armed robber. We got it all on *Cop Cam*. Here are some highlights now!'

'I'm hungry,' I interrupt.

Mom tuts at me, 'You just have to go out and get yourself something. We've got to conserve money on this trip, looks like it's going to be a long one.' She emphasises *long one* as if the immense distance from Orlando to North Dakota is anything to do with me.

'I thought you said money don't matter 'cause the Tribulation is at hand.'

Mom frowns through a cloud of smoke. She's not really listening. 'Less of that missy. There's $10 in my handbag. Don't spend it all.'

I pocket the money and go back outside, unsure what to do or where to go. It's five in the afternoon. We've hardly eaten all day. There's a small Chinese restaurant at the entrance to the motel but it's closed and doesn't look about to open anytime soon. The road stretches on. I don't recall seeing much as we drove up here, no McDonald's, no Subway, nothing. It's still so hot and my shirt and jeans are grimy. I've been wearing the same clothes for nearly two days now and I'm sweating just standing here. I want to wash my hair and my face and change my outfit because I just feel like this greasy streak of stink but I've had enough of Mom and whatever I do or wear she'll needle me about it. I also check my phone – I don't like to do it around Mom – but of course no one has sent me any messages. Why would they? I'm just a sad ugly freak with freak parents. Opposite, small kids continue to run around yelling at each other and the two fat men remain slumped drinking beer. No sign of the boy but I sense the men watching me. I walk across the road where there's nothing but trees and give Dad a call.

The phone rings a long time and then cuts out. I count to ten and try again. This time it's answered.

'It's me.'

'Esther, honey? Where are you?'

'Rome. Georgia.'

'Well I'll be. How's the trip going?' Typical Daddy. He always sounds like he just woke up, sort of dazed and not quite there. I could probably answer 'Rome, Italy' and he would have said just the same. That's my parents for you. Mom is loud and always rocking with the wrath of the Lord whereas Dad is much quieter, pacing about or 'atoning' as he calls it, reading passages from the Bible to himself, that sort of thing. Least he don't whip himself no more. That was a bad patch, Daddy out in the yard with his shirt off, lashing himself with his belt all the while muttering, 'forgive me Lord, forgive me Lord' until his back were a mess of welts and blood. It's all connected to the 'incident' which Mom and Dad don't care to discuss no more. I wish I knew what it was that was said to have happened, then I might better understand how we found ourselves in this mess. But I don't. I'm in the dark. 'Daddy,' I say, 'I think we ought to come home. I'm worried about Mom.'

'Your mother's always been like this hun. I'm counting on you to keep an eye on her.'

'Can you not speak to her? I don't think she knows what she's doing.'

'Me? Speak to your mother?' he starts to cough. 'Well now, I don't know about that. Your mother is a wilful lady Essie. She won't be spoken to. Not by me. Not by no man save the good Lord himself, praise be his name. We got to respect her gift.'

'I don't think she —'

'—Now, now Essie, your mother has been anointed. She's one of the most blessed, a prophet in service of the Lord.'

'But Daddy—'

'—No buts my precious lamb. You must open your heart and follow where she leads. Some of us are born to find the path and some to follow the pathfinder. We're all praying for the both of you.'

Daddy never stands up to Mom. For the millionth time I wish he'd never lost his job at Disney World. The 'incident' must have been pretty bad because he joined the church shortly after, him and Mom praying and crying, crying and praying every night as if enough tears and hallelujahs would make up for whatever it was that happened or 'didn't happen'. Dad got himself ordained as a junior minister and they pulled me out of school soon after and now all his time is spent in that church but Mom is the one with the real fever. She always had it, going on about End Times, the Rapture and the Tribulation even before the 'incident'. I've lost count of the occasions she would come down for breakfast claiming an angel had told her such and such in a dream or a vision. But her angels must all be crummy because their advice is never no good. Lately though, it seems as if her angels have all been telling her to go to North Dakota.

Angels, or else the guy who runs the blog, Earl.

I thumb through my phone to find Carly's number. She was my best friend till Mom took me out of school. I'm meant to be getting what they call 'home schooled' now but that don't seem to amount to much other than watching the local Christian cable channels. Just before we left I saw one where the host, the Rev. Shuttleworth, had this guy in talking about the Nephilim. He showed photos of stone monuments in places like England and Egypt that he said were made by giants, the giants being the Nephilim or their children or something. It's all in the Scripture apparently. All I can say is Scripture can be dull but this was interesting in a weird sort of way. Anyhow, Carly's phone goes straight to voicemail. 'Hi Carly,' I say. 'It's Esther. Mom's doing one again and we're on our way to North Dakota. It's the end of the world apparently. Give us a call if you get the time.'

I walk round and round the motel parking lot hoping Carly might get the message and call me back but she doesn't. I see a dead cat on the side of the road, flat and dry and half eaten up with maggots. *Yuck.* Not knowing what else to do, I cross over to the vacant lot next to the motel where I see the boy again. He just seems to be hanging round and looks my way and my face goes red. I want him to talk to me and at the same time I don't want him to. I'm so hideous, why would he even acknowledge I exist? But he's coming over. In a panic I take out my phone and pretend to check messages.

'Hey,' he says without really looking at me. I don't really look at him. 'Don't s'pose you got any smokes do you?'

I don't smoke. I've never smoked a cigarette. I just breathe the air around Mom. Instead, I shrug and say, 'Not right now no,' my face blushing even redder.

He looks away. He's squinting because the evening sun is so bright. Is he handsome? He's quite skinny. I wonder what it would be like to put my hand on his chest and lay my head against it. 'Why you here?' he says. He's seventeen, maybe eighteen years old. I don't even know why he wants to speak to me. I feel myself start to shake.

'I'm travelling with my mom. We're heading north to visit my grandma.' Truth and lie. 'How about you?'

'We're heading the other way. We came south from Iowa.'

'Oh.' I'm not sure what else to say. I press my hands tight together so he won't see me tremble.

'My dad calls us refugees. We've been stopped here for two weeks now.'

'Oh,' I say again then bite my tongue.

'He says there's a war between those that have been saved and those that have not.'

'Your daddy sounds like my daddy.'

'Are you saved?'

'I guess so. My daddy's a pastor in Florida so I must be.' That's another lie. Daddy is no pastor, not really. If he was, I don't reckon I'd be here. We'd probably be rich. There's a lot of people go to the church. I can tell the boy knows I'm not rich though, not when we're at an Economy Inn. We stand there a bit. I bite my nails then stop.

'Do you know if it's true?' I ask, speaking almost without thinking. 'What they say is happening?'

'Reckon so,' he nods. 'Before we left we saw lights in the sky three nights in a row.'

'My mom says she thinks the lights people is seeing is angels.'

'Have you seen them?'

'No.'

'They ain't angels.'

'Oh.' I want to ask what they might be but I don't. Instead I say, 'Is there anywhere to eat round here?'

The boy considers my question for a moment, all thoughtful-like. 'Not really. But there is a number for a pizza delivery place in reception.'

'Okay, thanks.' What else can we talk about? I try to imagine the boy kissing me but why would he kiss me? I've never kissed a boy. My face feels like it's on fire. I wish I was wearing nicer, prettier clothes, a dress perhaps but I don't have anything nice to wear. 'I have to go,' I tell him. 'Thank you.'

Idiot, I think to myself as I walk away. Why am I so stupid?

***

'Wake up!' Something wet and cold over me – what the? Sleeping but now awake. Mom is standing with an empty glass in her hand, all wild eyed, her hair a mess. 'Come on!'

'What's going on?'

'Get up you lazy little bitch. We need to pack, we need to go, we need to pack. For the love of Jesus, come on!'

I sit up in bed, my face and top all wet. I try to argue but Mom is flapping and shouting so I find myself stuffing my things back into a suitcase and then her things. She's pacing about. It's only five a.m., dark out. Mom makes a shushing noise. I see the .45 sticking out of the back of her jeans.

We hurry to the car, me carrying the suitcase, Mom looking this way and that. She pops open the trunk and I just about manage to heft the suitcase into it. A final look at the Economy Inn. I think about the boy who must still be sleeping in one of the rooms and who is travelling south not north. As we head along the main road I suddenly realise Mom didn't pay for the room. For a minute I think I'll ask her but it's better to imagine jumping out at the next red light and running back home. I could go live with Carly and we could fulfil our ambition of making it big on *YouthTube* with her singing and dancing and me writing the songs. But I don't go and live with Carly. I sit in the car and watch dawn light the sky.

***

For once we're making good progress on the Interstate. I try to relax and enjoy the scenery. It's not like we normally go anywhere. Depending on my parents' mood, America is either the greatest or the worst place in the world but I've seen so little outside Orlando that I think maybe this is a chance to judge for myself. The landscape changes but little else and after a while I get so tired of seeing the same drive-thrus, the repeated advertising hoardings and retail outlets that I start to have this weird feeling, like we're on a giant conveyor belt, as if the landscape is a projection, a screen and that none of us are actually going anywhere. Mom has the radio tuned to various Christian stations, trying to keep abreast of the news but there doesn't seem to be much mention of what's been happening. We're headed for a fracking town called Stanley far, far away in North Dakota.

Why? It must have something to do with the weird videos Earl posted on his blog, but that doesn't exactly seem like a good reason to me and anyway, I can't let on to Mom that I know about him. Mom tells me she had a series of dreams in which an angel told her the first of the seven seals had been broken. She said she dreamt three times of a white horse riding across the wilds of Dakota and the third time the horse had a rider, a giant with a bow and arrow and this, she said, was a clear sign. She didn't say why the first of the seven seals would be in North Dakota but those clips make it clear that something weird must be going down and it seems like the federal government has sent troops in to quarantine the place. Most people seem to think it's the Ebola virus which Mom said was a curse from God anyway. 'Just wait for the red horse,' she says, 'then we will know.'

Mom is able to interpret more or less anything as a sign. 'Look,' she said a couple of hours later as we passed a warehouse on fire in a lot off the Interstate: clouds of greasy black smoke rising upwards, red and yellow fire trucks all around. 'Look at that. I tell you doll, I'm getting Tribulation tremors.' Almost anything gives Mom what she calls 'tremors': could be Obama winning the election, could be war in the Middle East, could be stem cell research and the fact that we're all human-animal hybrids now, it don't matter.

Mom never gets hungry but around lunchtime my pestering pays off and we exit the Interstate and follow signs for a Walmart. Mom parks a long way from the store and tells me to go get us some food. The parking lot is mostly empty but there's no question of asking if we can park a little closer. Glancing back and flinching against the hot sun I see the silhouette of her hunched in the car, shoulders twitching as she works her phone. It takes Mom forever to send a text.

Truth be told, Mom's having an affair. Or not quite an affair, exactly, but she's up to something. I've been keeping an eye on her laptop and she's been having lots of G-chats with this Earl Landis guy who runs the *NewOathKeepers* blog. I've found hundreds of messages between Mom and Earl and okay, whilst it wasn't exactly like they were saying 'oh I love you', no, mostly it was long emails discussing the stuff Mom likes to go on about – government conspiracies, the End Times, the Illuminati, gun control, whatever – but lately I've seen a lot of talk about 'getting to know each other properly' and in some of them Mom has included pics of herself from the webcam wearing lots more lipstick and mascara than usual and kind of leaning forward in a way that shows off her cleavage and a lacy push-up bra. It's real embarrassing. If that wasn't gross enough the guy reciprocated with pictures of himself without his top on – he's sort of fat and very hairy – holding big guns in both arms and looking pleased with himself. He's very different from Dad, who is skinny with no muscles and not much body hair either. I've kept a close eye on his blog and he's been talking a lot about going to North Dakota to find out 'what's really going on', if it's the Second Coming or UFOs or some big government cover-up. In any case, even thinking about Mom and this guy makes me sick: he's obviously not a good influence.

I take my time, picking up some bread, cheese and sliced ham so we can make sandwiches and then it hits me – we're going to meet this guy, that's what this whole trip is really about; we're not going to Stanley, we're going to see Earl.

When I get back to the car Mom isn't on the phone anymore. She's just staring out the window looking sad with a cigarette almost burnt down to the ends between her fingers. My presence rouses her. 'Come on then, we can't dilly-dally,' she snaps.

I do my best to make us sandwiches as we head back to the Interstate. To my surprise Mom turns off the Christian station and finds one playing R'n'B. Normally, Mom would denounce this as 'godless trash' but today she taps her fingers to the beat. I quickly check my phone but Carly still hasn't replied to my call or texts. She was more or less my last friend in the world, but I guess she's decided to forget about me. I don't blame her. She always said Mom was 'one crazy bitch' and I have to agree.

'Doll.'

I can tell by Mom's tone that what she's about to say won't be good. I swallow a mouthful of sandwich and nod 'uh-huh?'

'We're not going to Stanley yet. We're going on a little detour.' I knew it! She tells me the name of a small town on the border of Missouri and Illinois and says we're going to a place near there called White Pines. I recognise the name from the *NewOathKeepers* website. 'Does Dad know about this?'

Mom sighs. 'Don't you worry about your father. You must understand things can be complicated sometimes. I know it all seems very simple when you're fifteen.'

'—It doesn't seem simple.'

'—But when you're older you'll understand. The good Lord will look after your father. Now, why don't you direct us to White Pines?'

***

Turns out I underestimated Mom's grasp of time and space. Turns out White Pines is only a hundred miles or so north of St Louis. Google maps got us so far then Mom handed me her phone. The guy had sent her some detailed instructions in a text.

Turns out White Pines isn't a real town at all and after we drove a long time along an isolated road past the odd farmstead and down a dirt track ('take a left by the rusty red tractor' said the text) which got narrower and dirtier with woodland on all sides, I find myself wondering what we're all in for. We bump and dip along the track for several miles before passing through an open gate.

Ahead, in a clearing in the woods I see three mobile homes. All three have satellite dishes and two have unlikely extensions tacked on using planks of wood and sheets of corrugated iron. Four pickup trucks and two mud splattered SUVs sit in the middle of the compound in a state of disrepair with trunks open, engines exposed and tyres removed. In the middle of it all is a flagpole, the Stars and Stripes rather forlorn in the still afternoon. No sooner has Mom turned off the engine when two Rottweilers come charging out of the largest trailer, shortly followed by a woman with something – a shotgun! – cradled in her arms. The dogs circle the car, growling and snarling and I watch, dismayed but somehow detached, as the woman – who is very overweight – struggles to raise the shotgun.

Is she actually going to blast us? I'm still wondering when a man pulls himself from underneath one of the pickups. 'Fidel, Castro heel!' he bellows. The Rottweilers hesitate, checked by their master's command. 'Put the gun down Betty for heaven's sake!' he yells at the woman. 'It's okay!' he smiles and waves at the car. I'm horrified to see Mom smile and wave back. The fat woman, 'Betty', lowers the shotgun. 'It's okay,' the man says to her again. He's covered in grease and dirt and is much chubbier than the photo suggested but it's him all right, it's the guy from the website, Earl Landis. 'Lauren!' he hails Mom, a big grin on his face, 'You made it!'

***

'Now, let me introduce you all to the family. The welcome party with the shotgun here is my wife Betty. She's territorial that's all. Betty, can you go and make us all some iced tea?' Betty grunts and goes back inside the trailer, taking the shotgun with her. A number of kids have emerged, the very youngest stumbling along in diapers while the oldest looks more like ten or eleven, but it's hard to tell as there are so many and they're all half naked, baked by the sun, covered in yard dirt and river mud. Earl does his best to introduce them, 'Noah', 'Jonah', 'Lisa-B', 'Earl Junior', 'Rebecca' and so on but they keep running off and reappearing, excited by our arrival or shy or something. 'And you've met my loyal buddies Castro and Fidel,' Earl gestures at the Rottweilers. 'They'll be fine with you now they got your smell. We've got a whole lot of other dogs here too, cats as well, all sorts of waifs and strays but don't worry 'bout them just yet. Look, here come the boys.' Two men are walking over from where they had been working with Landis on the pickup. 'Meet Frank and the big guy, that's Rawlins. Gentlemen, meet some new additions, Lauren and Esther.'

'Much obliged,' said Frank. He's sort of normal looking, stocky kind of guy, five nine, five ten, with close cropped brown hair and blue eyes, the sort of dude who probably used to play a lot of football at high school but since then has drunk a lot of beers and done very little exercise. He's in his late twenties, maybe early thirties, but to be honest my attention is bought up by the other guy, 'the big guy' Rawlins. He's six six, maybe six seven and he's ugly as a half-finished statue. He's not wearing any top and almost his entire torso is covered with tattoos: a swastika on one bicep, the symbol surrounded by flames and lots of smaller skulls coloured red and blue and – when he turns round – a huge iron cross on his back, with weird Gothic lettering above it. I didn't want to stare but it's hard not to. These didn't look like good tattoos to me. I mean, who has a swastika tattoo, right? He's really muscular, with massive arms and a chest that looks like it could take just about anything, and there's a sort of raggedy, mean quality about him as well, the way scars criss-cross his body as if he's been pushed through a mincemeat machine and then sewn back up again and the scars combined with the tattoos combined with the muscles make him look like a character from one of those Xbox games set in the future when humanity has been wiped out and all that's left are a few hard, desperate men to fight the robots. He's even wearing combat pants and sunglasses to hide his eyes. He doesn't even say 'much obliged' just looks us up and down and snorts as if to say when things get heavy Mom and I don't stand a chance.

'Rawlins is kinda crotchety,' laughs Earl. 'But he's just a big ol' softie really ain't that right?' placing an arm around his friend.

'Get the fuck,' mumbles Rawlins, shaking him off.

'Where's Sarah?'

'Hey Sarah, get your bony butt down here!' Rawlins yells.

'I'm coming.' A blonde woman emerges from the second trailer, facing the heat in cut-off denim shorts and a vest top. Like Rawlins, she's also covered in tattoos, the most impressive one I see – as she bends to pick up a child – a weeping angel across her shoulders in dark blue ink. 'Welcome to White Pines,' she says. 'Couple of these critters is mine. This is Rachel.' She gently bounces the little girl, naked apart from her diaper, up and down in her arms. 'That one over there is Eli – Eli stop doing that will you!'

'Oh such lovely children,' Mom gushes, cooing over them. I leave her to it and wander away. Someone shuffles out from the third trailer, the most broken-down of the three: an old guy with a fuzzy Santa Claus beard, one arm gripping a crutch as he negotiates the uneven ground.

'That there is Poppy Mac,' says Earl. 'Poppy,' he calls to the old timer, 'it's the folks I was telling you about, Lauren and this here is her daughter Esther. Lauren is a prophet in the service of the Lord.' But Mom is preoccupied with Sarah's kids.

The old man stands for a minute, as if contemplating this information. 'That one,' he says finally, pointing a wobbly hand at me. 'Come over.'

'Go on and say hi to the old man,' Mom urges. *Jesus, okay.*

His whole body is trembling as if it takes all his effort and willpower just to stand. He looks at me, lips quivering, his wet, toothless mouth opening and closing, 'Mmm... mmmm.' I smell old man smells: piss, sweaty clothes, booze, tobacco, gunpowder. 'Y-y-y-y-you had b-b-b-better m... m-m-m-m...' it's like he's vomiting parts of the alphabet and gets stuck at 'm'. I pretend to understand, nodding and smiling at him, 'Yes, yes,' I say pointlessly.

Thank God I can break off as Betty re-emerges from her trailer with a tray, glasses and a huge pitcher of iced tea. 'Would you like some?' I ask the old guy and without waiting for an answer peel back to Betty. A younger woman follows Betty out with more glasses. I watch her quite carefully. I don't think she could be much older than me – twenty, twenty-one? She's almost pretty, I suppose, with long dark brown hair that looks like it needs a wash (but who am I to judge?) and she's very skinny with no tits or hips at all, but her appearance is spoiled by her baffled expression, the way her mouth hangs open, a sort of perplexed glaze to her eyes that makes me wonder if she's stupid or, as Mom might say, 'touched by the Lord'.

Earl continues, 'This here is my other wife, Sue.'

Wait did he say his *other wife*? How many wives does this guy have? What is this, Utah? Does he want to make Mom his third wife? Oh God, are they all together in some disgusting sex thing? It's possible. Anything is possible.

Most people know what to expect from their parents. Not me, no sir, no such luck. My parents are liable to do just about anything. I keep looking at Mom to see if she disapproves – she ought to disapprove, she always does when this sort of crap is on TV – but she's just looking at Earl like he's some sort of golden jackpot and doesn't even seem to notice Sue or Betty.

'Anyway, here's the family,' Earl gestures at everyone, 'Betty, Sue, Rawlins, Frank, Sarah and Poppy Mac over there – Sue, help Poppy to his seat will you? We're one member short,' he's talking to Mom again, 'the Reverend Parker, Cornelius Parker, he's our authority on all matters scriptural but right now he's out on the road, spreading the word. He lives over yonder,' he gestures at the woods beyond the compound. 'He prefers the sanctuary of nature to the comforts of man. You'll meet him tomorrow I hope, or in the next few days anyhow. He's promising to bring us something special.' Earl pauses, takes off his cap and rubs some of the sweat from his face. I swat a mosquito. 'Anyway, we're all mighty happy to have you here.'

'Where are we sleeping?' I ask. It strikes me that, with all these people and animals there really isn't that much space at all.

'Good question. I set up a tent for you. And if you need to go in the night the outhouse is just over there. Best take a flashlight with you.' He points at a small tent pitched a little awkwardly on the sloping ground. I walk over and have a look. It's insanely hot in the tent and there's nothing inside but a dirty sleeping bag. I can just imagine all the bugs that will get me. I don't even want to look at the outhouse.

'Mom!'

'Come on honey.' Mom takes Earl's arm, 'It'll be like camping. Camping is fun right? You can always sleep in the car if you don't like it.' From the way she's clinging to Earl she looks like she won't be sleeping in any tent tonight. *Slut*. What do Sue and Betty make of it? For a minute I feel like I want to cry – how did this happen? It's all so unfair. I just want to be home. I just want a normal life. WHY ARE MY PARENTS SUCH FUCKING FREAKS?

'Oh honey, don't be like that. She's tired that's all.' Mom is steering me away from the tent and back to the trailer. 'The heat gets to her.'

'Have some tea sweetheart.'

I sit down and wipe my eyes and take the beaker of iced tea that Betty hands me. 'You'll be all right, we're all friends here. Things take a bit of getting used to, that's all,' and she glances, as she speaks, towards Mom. Now that she's not pointing a shotgun at us I decide she's quite nice, or at least she smiles at me as if to say, 'we're on the same side here'. Maybe she secretly hates Mom as much as I do and wants us to leave as much as I want us to leave? Perhaps she can help me out? I drink iced tea and sit and listen while the 'grown-ups' talk. Which is to say Earl talks, Mom laughs and Sarah joins in while Betty keeps an eye on the kids and Sue just sits, hugging herself, a 'back in five minutes' expression on her face. I notice Mom is having a beer rather than ice tea. She usually keeps her drinking secret – they don't tend to like it so much in the church – but I doubt anyone here will care. The two guys stroll back to the pickup they were fixing and the old man falls asleep in a deckchair. One of the kids takes a shine to me,

Lisa-B, a scrawny girl of about six who sits on my knee and gives me a little cross she's made out of twists of wire. She squirms about asking for cuddles and a couple of times Earl glances at me and says, 'That's a little angel of the Lord you've got right there Esther, if ever I saw one.'

'She's mine,' laughs Sarah. 'She's been saying she wanted a big sister weren't you Lisa-B?'

Rawlins walks up to our gathering carrying an assault rifle. 'Frank and I are going to start the barbecue. I'm going to see if I can't catch us some fresh game from the woods.'

'You won't shoot shit with that,' laughs Earl. 'Want to borrow my Blaser?'

'This'll do me fine.'

I must look worried because Sarah touches my knee. 'Don't you worry hun, Rawlins had his troubles in the past but there's no sinners can't be redeemed by the grace of our Lord. Reverend Parker shows us the way, you'll see that when he gets back. Your heart should be light because we are among the last.' She smiles at me like she really believes it. Rawlins slots a magazine into his assault rifle.

'Do you really think the Tribulation is coming?' I ask her.

'Oh you sweet little lamb, can't you see what your mother has shown you? The Tribulation ain't coming, it's already here.'

***

The afternoon unfolds, hot and slow: Rawlins disappears into the woods while Earl and Frank start the barbecue. After a while we hear gunfire. Everyone stops. Frank jokes with Earl, 'Stupid motherfucker won't hit shit,' but a little later Rawlins returns with a small deer bloody and dead over his shoulder. I try not to watch as he and Frank skin and strip the animal. The air is full of flies and the rancid smell of garbage left out for too long in the sun. Behind the trailers is a huge pile of old plastic bottles and other stuff. I keep hoping to get a moment alone with Mom but she holds fast to Earl, looking at him in a way that I never saw her look at Daddy and doing everything she can to avoid me.

I turned my phone off a while ago to conserve the battery. Now it's dark and as everyone is busy with the barbecue or keeping an eye on the kids, I wander into the woods and turn it back on. The air thrums to the sound of insects and the light from the screen casts blue shadows. I have little battery and no signal. I want to call Dad, tell him where we are and ask him to come and get me but even as I switch the phone back off I know that's also pointless and that he wouldn't do anything, even if I begged him. God's will or not, however he likes it. For the second time I feel like crying: it's all so unfair – why me? Why my parents? Why the incident? Why wasn't I born in Europe, somewhere like – I don't know – like Norway? I want to go and live in Norway. It looks nice over there, the fjords, the mountains, the cold, the sensible people who don't believe in the end of the world.

But it's no good and now I hear Earl shouting, calling everyone together. I walk back to the compound. 'You gotta check this out guys,' he's yelling while holding a laptop aloft. 'A new video came in an hour ago.'

I hang back as the others gather round but Mom ushers me forward. 'You ought to see this hun. You remember the one I showed you before.' Sure, I remember the footage. It's like one of those Trixxxie Foxxx black and reds, pretty much everyone in the USA must have seen it by now: the grainy footage of the lights in Colorado that hover mysteriously in the sky and then dip suddenly down, the voice that says 'sweet Jesus'. It sent the nation UFO crazy. Fox News even tracked down the couple who made the film and they swore it wasn't a fake. I saw the report Fox made about it – the couple, an ordinary middle-aged pair of steadfast Republicans – took the crew to see strange burn marks in the fields past their house and speak to farmers who talked about all the weird stuff that happened to their cattle. But what made the story so juicy, what really got everyone wound up was the fact that the couple disappeared shortly after: they vanished without trace leaving behind their car, their house keys, their credit cards and money. Fox said they were 'snatched from the surface of the earth'. A few weeks after two bodies were found not far from their house, burnt almost beyond recognition. I can't recall if DNA testing said it was them or not.

Earl sets the laptop on a table so everyone can watch. The footage is jerky – but it always is with these things – and it takes a moment to realise what we're looking at: a highway, traffic at a halt, red taillights in one direction, yellow headlights in the other and above, a twilight sky, traces of sunset lingering above a dark ridge. The audio is crackly but I can hear several excited voices and the camera swoops up, focusing on part of the sky and we see it. 'Will you look at that!' Earl exclaims: on the screen, lights, lots of lights, swirling together and then coming apart, that put me in mind of jellyfish, signalling to each other – it's beautiful, it's undeniably beautiful and Mom calls out, 'It's them angels, it's like I dreamt, angels in the sky, hallelujah!' On the film we hear the voices of the people watching getting more excited and the screen briefly turns around to focus on the guy filming, his sweaty face looming large as he exclaims, 'I don't believe it!' It's all blurry on the screen for a few seconds and when we swing back into focus it seems as if some of the lights are also rising from the ground but it's hard to tell they're so bright they distort the lens and as this is happening someone can be heard saying, 'My nose is bleeding,' and someone else says, 'So is mine,' and the guy filming shouts, 'Get back to the car, quick!' And then the screen goes dark.

No one says anything until Mom puts down her can of beer and starts muttering loudly, 'Oh my Lord, dear sweet Jesus, our father, who art in heaven,' while swaying backwards and forwards.

'Didn't look like no motherfuckin' angels to me. Looks like them vampires,' Rawlins grunts.

Now Sue is making a weird humming noise. 'No, not angels,' she mumbles, rocking back and forth, 'not angels.'

'Guide your sheep my Lord, oh guide us Jehovah, we who labour in darkness,' Mom keeps at it. Her shtick is so embarrassing but I know everyone in the compound will fall for it. They haven't seen her do this week after week in church like I have.

'Where did that come from?' Frank asks Earl.

Earl gives Mom a look of concern. 'One of my sources emailed it to me, Oath-Keeper, a state trooper in North Dakota.' He leans forward and lowers his voice slightly, as if anyone could overhear us. Even Mom shuts up for a minute. 'He says they found a dozen burnt out cars strung along the Interstate, like there had been some sort of accident. But he says none of the cars had crashed into each other. They'd all just burst into flames. Apparently the FBI was already on the scene. Already! I don't know how he managed to get the footage – it was off a cellphone they found dropped in the verge – but he did. I got to upload this shit to the blog. People are going to freak.'

'Are you sure that's a good idea Earl?' Frank wants to know.

'Truth must out Frank.'

'AND PROPHECY FULFILL!' Mom interrupts, bellowing and shaking all over. Oh my, she's really going for it this time. Her eyes roll up into her head and she starts chanting, 'ALLAWHALLA GABBA WALLA... OH LORD, OH LORD, HMM, HMMM... HMMM.'

'Is she all right?' shouts Sarah.

'She's fine, just ignore her,' I say but everyone ignores me.

'The spirit of the Lord is strong in this one!' Betty gets to her feet and takes my Mom's hand. I'm disappointed.

'She's speaking the language of angels!' Earl is real excited now.

'No she isn't. She's just making up noises.' Everyone continues to ignore me.

Mom drops to her knees and then from her knees she flops onto her side, making a sort of gagging, choking noise like a pregnant seal going into labour. She'll start vomiting soon. 'Give her air!' someone yells. All the kids are watching and one of the girls begins to cry. Little Rebecca looks at me as if she thinks I'm as crazy as Mom. Sue, who has been standing a little way off chooses this moment to fall to the floor as well and soon she's writhing next to Mom in the dirt as if this is some sort of competition. 'A black chariot!' Sue howls. 'A pale rider!' Mom adds.

'Just stop it Mom! Stop it!'

'You can't stop the Word of God, child.' Betty's holding Mom's hand as Mom starts the inevitable puking. Sue continues to writhe and moan next to her. 'Let it out dear, we are with you.'

'The valley of perdition!' Sarah hollers.

What's the use! I've seen Mom do this a thousand times and couldn't give a damn. They can all go to hell! Leaving everyone to tend to Mom I go and sit in the tent by myself. It's hot and horrible and dark inside and this must be the worst night of my life, the absolute worst! I can hear them all still carrying on and no one comes to check on me. They don't care and neither do I. Tomorrow, I vow to myself, no matter what it takes, I'm going to get out of here.

THE ABOMINATION OF DESOLATION

I meet a man in New Orleans who shows me the heart of a dead vampire. The man's name is Abraham Helsing and he is a good Christian man in a city so wicked that three times God tried to it wash from the surface of the earth and three times this city withstood God's wrath. I meet Abraham in a bar where the ungodly seek refuge from their torment in drink and fornication. We sit at the back by a machine that plays songs of damnation and loss and we drink tomato juice. The man has a briefcase and in the briefcase is a box and in the box is the heart of a dead vampire. It is a shrivelled thing, shrivelled and brown and withered as all evil withers eventually, but I can smell the stench of the Beast all over it.

'You can kill a vampire, if you have a big enough gun and a sharp enough knife, you can do it,' says Abraham as I sniff and prod the heart. 'I killed this one.'

'I have no need of weapons. God is my sword, prayer my shield.'

'That right? The Lord and I talk often enough but prayer won't do shit if you're up against a vampire full of blood-rage. It's like I says to my wife Carlene...'

I had no desire to know what he says to his wife Carlene. I ask the man what he wants for his vampire heart. He looks a little bashful and paws at his bald head. 'This one, you see,' he begins, 'this one was a real tough mother, if you'll forgive my language. A second generation half-blood, true name Azathoth. He'd been on this earth about six thousand years before he met me.' The earth is only five thousand years old but I can't be bothered to correct him. He says the going rate for a heart is between $20,000 and $50,000 but as this one was old and 'more or less dead' he would settle for $15,000. I ask what a 'new and alive' heart might be but he will not be drawn. 'They never exactly die,' is his answer. 'And even when you think they might be dead, might be dead for years and years, they can still come back, a bit like when you find an old car battery in the garage you reckon is a goner and then you hook it up right and boom.' I tell him I don't drive and that I am a servant of the Lord and that these are the End Times when no true Christian would seek to profit from such evil. I tell him money will be useless when the righteous are Raptured and the rest left to face the anti-Christ. I tell him these vampires are demons, part of Satan's horde from the Fall and that if they are free to roam the earth it is part of God's will, His way of telling us that the Tribulation is at hand. As I speak I look deep into this man and I see a good man who has struggled for a long time on a path that is lonely and hard. 'You are not a glory seeker,' I say to Abraham, 'but you deserve your share in the everlasting glory.'

Abraham mops his sweating brow. 'Well I guess I can sell it to you for ten, you being a man of the cloth and all.'

'Eight.'

'Well, all right then,' he holds out his hand, 'you got yourself a deal.'

I nod and tell him I have to make a phone call. I leave the bar and find a payphone on the street outside. I call Earl and when he answers I instruct him to transfer $10,000 into my account immediately. Eight for the heart, two for expenses. He says he will. 'Earl, I'm concerned about you, I fear you have been unduly swayed by the temptation of false and low women.' I vow that on my return to White Pines there will be a mighty scourging and a reckoning. There can be no backsliders among the armies of God.

I go back inside and tell Abraham I will have the money for him tomorrow, at eight in the morning. He shows me where to meet and I promise to pray for his soul.

***

When I leave the bar a second time I am aware that a man in a brown shirt shadows my path on the other side of the street. Perhaps the man expects me to lead him to a hotel or some such place but he will be disappointed because this man will give up before I have need of rest. My name is Cornelius Parker but most people simply call me 'the Reverend Parker' and the wrath of God is with me. Verily, I walk the streets of this accursed city. I walk past the rich man's mansion and the poor man's shack and both languish in the anguished darkness of sin and the generation of sin. I walk through the French Quarter and see the drunkard and the harlot, I see the whore, the dealer and the beggar, I see them all, peddling their wares on the street when they should be in church begging the Lord for mercy. I see the fake churches for the false Christians and I think of the Lord and the message Christ left us. I think of the parable of the fig tree and how by tender branch and sight of the leaves upon the boughs we may know that summer is nigh. I know there shall be signs in the sun and signs in the moon and signs in the stars, signs upon the earth, in the distress of the nations, in the angry seas and in the roaring waves. This is it: the end of history has already been written and is in the Scripture for every man to read. There can be no surprises for God and no surprises for those who understand the word of God. I see it all now, see it so clearly, the motions of divine providence. Jesus said there will be false Christs and false prophets and this has come to pass. Jesus said there would be calamity upon calamity – flood and famine, war and strife, pestilence and fire – and all this has come to pass. What will happen has all been foretold and it will be much worse than the environmentalists can envisage, much worse than anything a scientist could conceive, worse than any educationalist or politician has words to explain. We face great strife and much gnashing of teeth. What, after all, is human history but the outcome of sin and the curse of God that humanity brought upon itself? It is right that we should suffer, right that we should see these things.

As I walk I look at the ugliness of raw sin and I think how the cup of indignation will burn it all away. I think of the righteous fire, the holy fire that will cleanse the world and my voice shakes as I sing and my eyes weep tears for the grace of God and for the mercy of Jesus. With an anguish of the spirit I fall to my knees and crawl on my belly low as the serpent that first brought man down. I crawl to a church to beg God for mercy but the church is closed and those who have fallen into the snare of Satan sit in the churchyard laughing, drinking and fornicating. I watch them make of the church a nest for their sin, an abomination of desolation where the mercy and grace of our Lord is mocked and profaned. They jeer and throw cans of Coke and beer at me even as I pray for their redemption and beg them to turn to the light. Yea, for these are the days of vengeance, these vampires another sign Tribulation is at hand. As was written, in the last days and times Satan shall be given the privilege of releasing all the demons bound from hell and they shall run rampant over the earth in one last mad dash against God and Christ. Tomorrow, I will have the heart of a devil and with it I will launch a revival such as the world has never seen.

Needless to say, when I remember to check, the man in the brown shirt follows me no longer.

***

At dawn I find myself where I had arranged to meet Abraham: a parking lot on the fringes of the city. Factories and warehouses of unknown design lurk on the horizon while the first aeroplanes of the day come in low to land at the nearby airport. Their engines howl with the rage of those who travel but cannot escape their sin. I sit on the asphalt, close my eyes and meditate on Jesus. After a while it is time. There is Abraham, parking his SUV in the lot.

'You all right buddy?' he says when he sees me. 'You look all in.'

'I'm fine.' I remove my hat to wipe my brow.

We sit in the air-conditioned comfort of his vehicle and he gives me some water. In my holy fury I realise I quite forgot to get him the money so I instruct him to drive me to the nearest ATM. The crisp $100 bills lurk in my wallet like little slithers of Sin.

'I was going to get some breakfast. You want some breakfast?'

I do. We sit in a diner and eat ham and eggs washed down with mugs of weak black coffee. Abraham tells me about his wife, Carlene. I'm just grateful the dizziness has passed. These nights with the Lord take their toll.

'What you going to do with it?' Abraham asks as he pours more coffee. I've got the box on my knee. It's perhaps more of a casket than a box, made of heavy dark wood with elaborate metal clasps that make a reassuring *snap* when opened or closed. The box is engraved with carvings of a large cross on every side. It's heavy and Abraham has fashioned a small handle and shoulder strap to make it easier to carry.

I take time to consider his question. 'I shall use it in my preaching. I shall show it to the people. Sometimes the people need something more than pure faith. We call on them to have faith but they have so little. Sometimes they need a sign, a most tangible sign, in order to show them clearly what it is that is happening. This,' I place my finger firmly on the box, 'this will be the sign.'

'So you'll what, take it out at the pulpit?' He looks doubtful.

'Indeed sir, if that is what is required, indeed I shall.'

'You know...' he hesitates. 'You got to be careful with them things. It's like I said to you yesterday. They never exactly die, not entirely, if you see what I mean...'

'Are you saying that one can be resurrected? Without a body?'

'Not exactly. I'm just saying, be careful. I kept that one in a deep freeze in my cellar. They like blood, do vampires. They like it a lot.'

I have the impression Abraham wants to say more. 'I appreciate your counsel,' I discover there are tears in my eyes and I wipe them away. 'Behold.' I smile and show him my tears. 'These times provoke a bittersweet emotion, do they not? Bitter, for those who do not belong to the Lord shall perish in a lake of fire but sweet for those – like us – who tread the path of righteousness and shall take our rightful place beside our Lord. Listen to me, Abraham, it is a glorious thing to think of Christ's return but it is also a frightening thing, is it not?'

'I guess.'

'Yes, yes it is. It's frightening because he comes not only to establish His kingdom but to judge the ungodly, and this will be a horrific judgement.'

'The lake of fire, I gotcha.'

'Yes sir, indeed! But with this demonical heart I will sway the doubters and, I hope, save many a wretched soul.'

'All the same, watch out, that's all I'm saying. Prayers and whatnot is all very well, but a vampire, well it's a whole different story.'

I shake Abraham's hand. 'God bless you.'

I leave the diner and start to walk along US-61, past the airport, past the city limits. Traffic roars by, constant and indifferent. No one else is walking. Carrying the box with the heart under my arm I will follow the Mississippi back to St Louis and from there to White Pines. When I get back with this proof Earl can post it on his blog and then we will hit the road, marching together unto glory and the greatest revival the world has ever seen! 'Hallelujah!' I proclaim, singing to the indifferent highway, 'Hallelujah, hallelujah!'

***

The Gospel tells us that he who abides with the Lord must walk like the Lord and so I walk all day. All day I walk and I am not weary. My thoughts stray, at times, to my false father, my 'real father' as the world would have it: that broken, weak man, a man so in need of the light and mercy of God and yet so frightened to leave the dark. Mother said it wasn't his fault, that it was the war that broke him, too many dead children in Vietnam but those children sure made Father drink, drink enough to wash Mother away. Good riddance, Father said when we went out to salute the flag each morning. He loved America but he had no love for Jesus. I remember him on Veterans Day, up before dawn to press and crease his old uniform, polish the medals, little sips from a silver hip flask full to help him through, standing stiff to attention as the parade went by and each evening the flask replaced by the bottle and I would seek refuge in the church because Father, for all his sin, respected the priest and would not come for me there. But Father is long dead now and shall not rise again.

***

As the sun starts to go down I find myself walking between the Mississippi – which lies past yonder fields – and the fringes of an industrial zone, a veritable Pandemonium of refineries and chemical plants, storage tanks and the rusting metal arcs of connecting pipes and tubes. I leave the road and wander through a field until I come to a suitable cluster of trees. Here I shall pass the night. I'm still unable to see the Mississippi but I can sense the impress of so much passing water. I whisper a quick prayer – glory to God in all his manifest majesty!

In addition to the heart in its box I have a small rucksack and from it I extract a waterproof mat and thus comforted I stretch myself out. The night is warm, I shall have no need of fire for aught except light but it seems prudent to hide myself from the eyes of outsiders. Although all this land is God's land and one cannot trespass on the inheritance of our true Father I know there is always the danger of others who see things differently. In any case, I will need only three or four hours of sleep before the righteous fury of God has me on my feet again.

The sky is as red as the blood drunk by these demons. Time, I think, to inspect my purchase. I open the box and extract the heart therein. The demon slayer was named Abraham. This cannot be a coincidence.

The heart is far larger than the heart of a man, perhaps four times and it is hard and brown and leathery like an old football and almost the same weight. Hanging underneath, as gnarled and knotted as old roots are what look to be small, calcified tendrils. For a moment, I wonder if it is the same as the heart Abraham showed me in the bar or if he might have switched it. Perhaps I've been too trusting? But no. The more I look the more clearly I can see: it is indeed a dread thing, radiant with malice. It also looks like a very real thing, solid and material, almost natural. But I know this is a satanic illusion. I know that which I hold is truly fashioned from a spiritual material. When the angels were expelled from heaven, their fall hardened their skin and turned it from an ethereal substance into this weighty matter. The very materiality of the heart is the clearest sign of its sinful condition.

I also have to admit it isn't very impressive, at least to those who might be less sensitive to its infernal vibration. I can imagine the sceptics pouring their scorn upon it: 'It could be anything,' they are certain to say. It is lumpy, ugly, indistinct, inanimate. I wonder about Abraham's words. What did a vampire need? Blood, of course, lots of blood. Perhaps I must try to coax just a little of this evil back to life? Murmuring a prayer, I take out my pocket knife and make the smallest of cuts in my left thumb. Tiny drops fall onto the heart. For a giddy moment I wonder if it's possible to cleanse it with my holy blood? Perhaps the righteousness of the true believer will purge the heart of evil and allow it to be reborn as the heart of an angel? To think – I would have birthed a seraphim. Ha, but no... foolish me. These are sentimental thoughts and surely not part of our Lord's providence. I watch as droplets of my blood run over the organ. Do I feel the faintest pulse from within the heart? No, 'tis nothing but the pressure of my own fingers, the echo of my own heart, pounding with excitement. I suck my wound and return the heart to its casket.

The sun is almost down. I realise I'm hungry and having finished my water long ago I'm thirsty too. God's grace will have to sustain me. In any case, it is right that I suffer. A final prayer and I close my eyes. Now, I much prefer to sleep under the canopy of heaven than to be confined in the boxy little house of man, but no matter how fatigued my body it always takes me a long time to relax, so heated is my brain with fervour for the Lord. Tonight, however, no sooner had mine eyes closed than I found myself dreaming; a red desert, a hot wind, afar, on a small hill, a glass house I sought to get to even though I knew that terrible, profane acts were being committed therein; I knew also that the whole world watched these acts, secretly, and secretly the whole world rejoiced in them. Towards the end of the dream, the sight of a man crossing the desert on a white horse and behind him the armies of the black flag and then I was pulled back to consciousness by the sun burning hot on my face.

I sit up and realise I'm drenched, not in dew, but a fresh layer of sweat. How can it be that the sun is so high in the sky? I check my watch and check it a second time in disbelief. Almost noon. How have I slept for fifteen hours straight? It's not possible. Yesterday's exertions must have exhausted me beyond all reason. All the same, I gather myself, change into my other shirt, collect the box (did it feel a little heavier?), return to the road.

I feel different, the hunger of the night before having translated itself into a more driving sort of need. I walk fast. My thumb, I notice, is quite sore – an angry red mark to show where the blade had been.

I walk along a straight road through a settlement called Geismar passing clusters of suburban bungalows, a large, newly built high school set far back across an open lawn, gas stations and car dealerships, retail strips and empty lots and it all swelters under the hot southern sky. These are the flatlands, the Badlands, the green wasteland of the American soul and there is no one about.

I walk for a long time before I see the McDonald's, yellow arches visible across the wide-open road. Sight of it makes me suddenly faint and very much in need: inside, the McDonald's is deliciously cool and empty, the floor has been mopped and there is the strong smell of bleach in the air. I order four Big Mac meals and go large on the lot. Then I find a booth and start to eat. I don't remember much: there's food in my mouth, a true American feast, food I hardly needed to chew, food that seems designed to stuff and swallow, stuff, swallow, gorge and slurp: the hot fatty sumptuousness of the burger, the crisp bite of the fries and gallons of Coke, the cool fizzy sweetness running into my teeth and through me like wet electricity. The yellowish smell of it: repellent and inviting at the same time. A glorious, intoxicating wash of salt, fat and sugar. I sit and I eat and I eat and I eat.

Afterwards, more than a little nauseous and keeping the box under my arm, I make my way to the bathroom. Water is applied to my forehead and I take refuge in the cubicle where I proceed to burp and fart copiously, ashamed to realise that in my gluttony I forgot to say grace before the meal. My ancestors in the Plymouth colony would have scourged themselves for less so it is only right God should punish me with a blast of damnable heartburn, only fitting that in my discomfort I should open the slit on my thumb and allow a little more blood to fall on the heart. It remains, as it was, a dry, leathery assemblage, as inanimate as mud. Strangely, though, the cutting seems to have helped: my head clears as the blood trickles, nausea passing as when clouds gather on a summer's afternoon and hint at rain only for the greater heat of the season to banish them to another day. I remember the Scripture: 'I am with thee, be not dismayed for I am thy God, I will strengthen thee, I will help thee and I will uphold thee with the right hand of my righteousness.'

I catch sight of myself in the mirror and see a man in his late forties, his hair thin and grey, his nose, ears and forehead burnt red by the sun; a man with tired blue eyes and three days of stubble on his chin. A man who has dirt around his dog collar and a suit that was once white but is now faded and yellow with the road, a man whose feet are sore and blistered, whose shoes are coming apart at the seams and whose legs and back ache with the weight of treading for so long on a hard road. I see all: I see this weary, broken man and I know it does not matter. The Lord cares not for my complexion. The Lord cares not if my armpits have been perfumed. He cares only for the spiritual body, the body within. He will uphold me with His righteousness.

Truly, the Lord watches over me. No sooner do I leave the restaurant when a good Christian trucker, tending to his rig, offers me a lift. As I climb into the cabin he tells me he is going as far as Memphis and this, as I tell him, is perfect.

On the road the man says his name is Simon Goodson. 'A good son you are indeed.' My joke provokes a smile from my driver. Simon tells me he drives freight, 'between Memphis and all points south'. He's married, I gather, with three children – their picture is on the dashboard next to the satnav – as his idle chat, combined with the heat of day, the motions of the rig and the glut of McDonald's like a slug in my belly soothes me and despite my epic sleep the night before I soon doze off. I dream, I think, of Apollo – a centaur with the body of a white horse – firing burning arrows towards the glass house in the desert and when I wake again we are deep in Mississippi, the road cutting through the green wilderness. It's almost dark and I wonder how the day left us so quickly.

Simon notices I've woken up and starts to ask me about football and who might win what. He is a supporter, of some kind, a sports enthusiast. 'I know nothing about this,' I snap. 'This is not the time for idle chatter. These are the last times, my good man.' I see the centaur; I see the burning arrow in the desert. 'What cares God with his flaming sword for the petty tournaments of man?'

'Oh, I'm sorry Father. I was just making conversation.'

Conversation indeed. My nap has left me in a curious mood. I feel as if a preaching is upon me. I ask Simon has he seen the signs, is he aware of the lights in the sky? He says he is but I sense he's lying. I tell him about the Scripture, that this gospel of the Kingdom shall be preached all over the world and then the end will come: the end is upon us, I say, repent, I say, repent that we might be saved. Simon tries to tell me he's been saved too, but I tell him it is a false Christianity in this land, that they worship the wrong Jesus, the unworthy God. 'Do you worship the true Jesus, Simon? Or do your prayers secretly go to Satan?' At this, he looks abashed and I can tell he wants to tell me his church is 'just fine' so I tell him that fallen angels, once buried deep within the earth, now walk among us as demons and I have proof. 'I have it,' I say, rapping the casket, 'just here, the heart of one. A vampire, we might call it.'

'You what?'

'Look,' I show him. Why not? If the heart will not impress upon him the urgency of the times, then with whom shall it work? Simon glances in the box, then back at the road, then at the box again and then the road. He seems troubled. The heart sits there, as always, dried up and brown, like a coconut. I know what he's thinking. That I'm pulling his leg and in a minute I'll burst out laughing and say, 'A vampire heart, good Lord you sure are gullible,' and we shall laugh.

Instead, I tell him this: 'Simon, I know you are a true Christian man. Believe me when I say I hope you've made your peace with the Lord, really I do. Look, why don't you touch it? It's real, you can see for yourself.'

'Touch it?'

'That's right.'

'Aw, I'm not sure about that now...'

'Why? You're afraid to touch the heart of wickedness? You should be. It is a fearful thing. But think man, think. We can't know the good unless we've known evil. Anyway,' I add rather hurriedly, 'this is but an artefact, an unholy relic. God watches over us and protects us from it.'

Simon reaches out and quickly puts his hand on the heart. 'Kinda soft,' he says, withdrawing almost immediately. He looks at his hand a moment, as if the skin might be sticky, and quickly returns it to the wheel.

Strange that he should describe the heart so. 'Is it not hard?' I say watching as Simon – almost despite himself – places his hand on it again.

'Weird.' A pause. 'It actually feels sort of nice.'

'Nice?'

He doesn't answer, just gives a strained sort of laugh, a laugh that seems to acknowledge the absurdity of it all, but that also shows how nothing else is to be done. 'Sort of nice.' I put my thumb in my mouth and taste my blood. We sit in silence, Simon's left hand is on the heart, his right on the wheel, truck headlights illuminating the empty straights ahead.

After a while he says, 'Father, I want to confess. I've seen bad things. I even done bad things, may the Lord forgive me.'

'It's all right,' I answer, wondering if I can stop him before he goes too far. My head is too weary for yet another man's tale of sin. 'God forgives you.'

'I was in Iraq,' he's babbling. 'Just the regular army. I did two tours of duty, first during the invasion and then in 2005. Baghdad, Ramadi, Fallujah, I went to all them places, saw a lot of combat.' His hand stays on the heart.

I remember my father in the darkened front room, drunk and filled with self-pity and the sin of self-hate.

'Don't trouble yourself so...' I mumble but he's away.

'We killed children,' he says. 'We killed a lot of kids.'

I want to tell him that these wars are another sign: Israel, Iraq, Islamic State, Syria, it's all been foretold. The Muslims think so themselves, they just read the signs differently. We're all pawns in the war between God and the Devil. Jerusalem shall be surrounded by armies. Angels will walk the streets of Damascus.

Simon is talking. 'At the time I didn't feel anything. But now, when I think back...' He removes his hand from the heart.

I'm not sure what he wants me to say so I elect to say nothing. What succour can I give this man? I'm not here to peddle soft illusions. I'm here to bring the heart of a demon to the world. What is this man's conscience set against the wrath of the righteous Lord? 'There will be a burning sword,' I tell him, 'and a scourging fire.' I close the box and hold it to me. It has started to rain, water dashes the windows and we drive on.

Around midnight we reach the outskirts of Memphis. 'Where do you want me to drop you?' Simon asks, the first words either of us has spoken in over an hour.

'The road will be fine. I must continue to St Louis. North of there, in fact.'

'Not tonight you ain't. Look at that rain.'

Simon has a point. The rain is severe. All of a sudden the idea of a motel seems very good indeed. We continue along the Interstate and follow directions to a place called the Applewood Inn. A two-storey structure appears out of the night, a 'vacancies' sign clearly available.

'This looks good.'

'Father—' he starts as I prepare to leave.

'Reverend,' I say, 'Reverend Parker. It will be all right son. I will pray for you.' I squeeze his arm and – avoiding his eye – quickly leave the truck.

I'm shown to a room that is comfortable and cool with double beds. Enough space for the Son, the Father and the Holy Ghost as I joke to the bellhop. Now he's gone and I'm alone.

The thumb, I fear, is no longer sufficient so I use the knife to make a small cut on the wrist of my left hand and I let the fresh blood flow onto the heart. I feel such a relief as I do this, as if a burden is being lifted from my shoulders. A little later, with a towel wrapped around my wrist, I lie back naked on the bed and fall into a deep sleep, the heart in its box, just inches from my head.

I wake at four a.m. burning with thirst and devour the two cans of Coke from the mini bar. Then I go back to sleep and wake hours later, groggy and desperate to urinate. The shower restores me a little. It's after nine and I must get going. All night the casket was open and when I check on the heart I have a desire to touch it and yes, it does seem a fraction softer, a little moist. But perhaps it's just the heat? The air conditioning stopped working and now the room is stuffy and close. I think it best to close the box and when I do it occurs to me that there should be bloodstains, inside, but I don't remember seeing any. I think about opening it again to check but decide not to. Those clasps should stay down and I must stop thinking about the heart and start walking for the glory of God.

Except this morning the righteous fury of the Lord is lacking and by twilight I'm still in the northern suburbs of Memphis. I got lost, I think, avoiding the centre but struggling to tell the way out of the sprawling city, where there are parking lots and trees, and red hued buildings set back from wide roads without traffic and men, on corners, who sometimes call out but are too lazy with the heat to do anything. The day passes, there are hours like this when I feel as if the Lord is far from me as I try to navigate by His distant star. And yet, for the second time I find myself in a McDonald's, eating three Big Mac meals and then retreating to the toilet to cut my wrist and feed the heart. I tell myself that I don't need to do it, that the heart is a dead thing, that I have done enough but then I find the knife, I open the wound and the heart is there. I do this: several times I do this, always planning to say no. There are never any bloodstains. I flush the toilet and splash water on my face. I am ready; we must go.

***

For three days and three nights it is the same. I walk all day, stopping now and then to open the wrist, to feed the heart. At night I lie in the bushes and dream three times of the centaur in the glass house sodomising a harlot woman while the armies of the black flag assemble in the red desert around them. On the third morning I am ashamed to discover I am no better than Onan; I have ejaculated, my pants are sticky with seed. Only the cutting and the feeding makes it any better. I don't have any more clothes and the incident bothers me, the congealing mess somehow worse than the layers of sweat, grime and country dirt that cover my clothes and sun-blasted skin. 'Why did you do that to me?' I mumble at the heart. 'You should know better than that.' I've taken to discoursing with it, as if the heart is my own familiar. The heart, I reason, is part of God's plan; it can't be anything else. There are no surprises for God: he is everywhere, all the time, he sees everything. He knows what will happen, knows if I will dream of the centaur or stop here to eat four Big Macs and then cut myself in the toilet – he knows this before I do. He knows that when I reach the outskirts of a small town with the pleasant name of Blytheville I will stop at the cluster of motels on the outskirts and go to the nearest one.

The receptionist is clearly appalled by my appearance and odour and tells me they only have an 'executive suite' available. I don't blink as I say yes and my bank card is still good. As I look around and observe the spacious and well-furnished reception, I realise this motel is actually a hotel, more upmarket than I first thought. It must be the best place in town.

My room is luxuriously appointed: there is a separate lounge with a large wooden desk and a sofa and there are two sinks in the bathroom, for him and her. 'Or for me and the heart,' I mumble to myself, trying not to smile and trying not to feel delight – for was not Jesus born in a manger and not a palace? I should be humble. Yes, it is important to be humble. How can one be close to Jesus in a suite? But after three nights in the bushes I'm glad to peel off my clothes and call down for laundry service to take them away and have them cleaned. I need this. I wrap myself in a cotton hotel bathrobe and inspect the damage: my face and neck boiled pink by the sun, peeling spider webs of skin marking the boundaries between the scorched regions and the rest; I have an itchy beard, flecked with grey and my feet are bleeding and torn, rubbed with blisters, itchy red swathes of athlete's foot between the toes and a fresh verruca on my left sole. My shoes are also worn, the soles coming off, their battered condition witness to how I have lived my life to Jesus' word. Searching myself I find numerous small bruises and cuts, dozens of mosquito and insect bites, some swollen, some oozing; the pain in my ass and blood in my waste suggest piles and there's a red rash all over my skinny behind and crusted layers of dried blood now cover the cut on my wrist. Like the saints of old I have mortified my body for the Lord but now I must retire and repair – my calling is not to extinguish myself in these exertions but to work a mighty revival and for that, I must restore my strength.

With a groan, I lie back on the bed; oh, it is very heaven! Such comfort – as if I bask on the wings of angels. Mounted on the wall opposite the bed is a huge flat screen TV. I do not normally watch television, not even the Christian channels – I consider most so-called 'televangelists' nothing but frauds, hypocrites the lot! Using the word of God as a vehicle for their own vanity and celebrity, to gain access to women – even men – yes, using the word of God as a doorway to depravity and the fulfilment of their own filthy desires. Shame. Shame on them all! True men of God do not stand and preach in front of a television camera. True men of God do not have a 'verified' Twitter account or a credit card hotline number. No, a true man of God labours in darkness and obscurity to bring the truth to light. That's what I shall do, with this heart. These televangelists are fake Christians, part of the satanic media upon whom they depend to spread their false message and inflate their egos.

The true man of God needs not the media: for the true man of God the message is Truth and Truth needs only itself to spread, for Truth – like this heart – is self-evident.

The other thing I don't like about modern televisions is just how complicated they are. I locate three separate remote controls. At random I try pressing what looks like the on button with each device while pointing them at the screen. The third attempt yields a pleasing buzz, the screen revealing a Cable Menu of channels listed in alphabetical order. First in the list are ADULT 1, ADULT 2 and ADULT EXTREME FANTASY. I should have known! In a panic I fumble madly, pressing all sorts of buttons, anything to get away from this nefarious trap. Too late! The screen flashes up 24 HOURS ACCESS ONLY $19.99 CONFIRM? Before I know it, the confirmed button flashes – PAYMENT ADDED TO ROOM BILL – Lord preserve us! And like that, I'm in. It's easy, the snare of Satan, it can catch anyone.

On the screen is a woman of such perfidy that even I have heard of her – Trixxxie Foxxx – denounced in many a pulpit as the whore of Babylon. She's standing there, flagrant and brazen in nothing but a skimpy thong and tiny bikini top: I can see the tattoo of a serpent running up one of her shapely legs and another at the base of her back – marks of the Devil, a demonic woman sporting the brand of Satan. I watch appalled as she turns her body this way and that, sticking her behind in the air and mewing like a cat, spreading her legs and arching her back; I watch, appalled, as she performs obscene acts with two burly men. The motions of this infernal Eve touch the base Adam within me – naked and fallen as I am – and my penis, like the serpent in Eden, is hard and throbbing with temptation and much as I despise myself I submit to a frenzy of self-pleasure. I know I should just turn off the television – but which controller and besides, it is too late now. On the screen the men ejaculate over Trixxxie and she snarls and shakes like the slut she is while I stand, my penis jiggering as I reach for the casket. I pull it onto the bed, unlock it and then, leaning forward, I groan and shudder all over the demon heart, dripping white globes of my holy fire. 'Get thee Satan, get thee!' Finished. The orgasm has overwhelmed me. Oh Lord. I roll back and collapse into deepest slumber.

***

I jolt awake, sit up and struggle to think of an appropriate quote from the Bible but my mind is blank and for a moment I can't recall a single word of Scripture. In the beginning was... and the Lord something... something? I'm perhaps disorientated because the television is still on, another film from the adult channel, two Sapphic succubae engaging in strange practices. There, that's the button... I'm relieved to turn it off.

Without looking inside, I close the casket and put it on the other side of the bed. There is an extensive room service menu and I order two large sirloins, 'as red and bloody as can be'. I'm so hungry. The food comes and I eat my steak, stuffing down one mouthful after another. The second steak I put in the box with the heart. I think of it mixing together, my blood and sperm and the juicy steak. I'm trying to work a miracle, I think, a miracle so that souls may be saved, so that as many as possible will turn to Christ before it's too late. But I tread a long hard path and right now it seems easier to recline on this bed and let my thoughts drift. I can hardly keep my eyes open... I dream about my father. We're sitting at the dinner table and he's telling me there are three types of people, 'sheep', 'sheep-dogs' and 'wolves'. He holds my hand tight as he tells me all this. 'Which one are you son, because let me tell you, I ain't raisin' no sheep in this house.' I'm a sheep-dog, I tell him, I'm a sheep-dog helping to shepherd my flock on the paths of righteousness. When I wake up it's still dark and I lie there trying to remember when my father said this. Then I realise he never did. It's a scene from the movie *American Sniper*. Rawlins and Frank love that film. They watch it over and over in White Pines. My father never said that. He never said anything like that to me. I almost wish he had. As I lie there I'm aware of a faint noise in the darkness – perhaps it's connected to the air conditioning – a faint churning, grinding sound... but no sooner have I noticed it than I'm asleep again.

***

In the morning, my clothes are delivered to the room, clean and pressed and accompanied with a note listing items (all of them, in fact) that were already damaged and noting 'some stains could not be removed'.

Still naked, I take the casket to the toilet and open it to look at the heart. There it is. But the steak I gave it last night is gone. There's not even a stain. Wait... am I remembering this correctly? 'What are you doing to me?' I whisper. 'Are you a treacherous heart? Are you?' It takes a few minutes before I'm able to reassure myself that I'm not making this up. Two food trays sit in the room. I ordered two steaks. I didn't dream it. I gave one of the steaks to the heart and it's not there anymore. I reach down and touch it. 'Are you a false heart?' Does it feel slightly moist, a little greasy? As my hand lurks on the craven device, I feel a sort of tug between the eyes through to the back of my head, as if there is a ribbon that is lightly pulled through my mind so that I see a great desert, a house of glass atop a crimson pyramid, a wind, a voice chanting... I open my eyes and let go. I'm back in Arkansas. Thank you Lord, I whisper, for this proof of your guidance. I place the open casket on my knee and hold my wrist over it. A little pressure from the knife opens the familiar wound all too easy.

Later, I'm dressed, breakfasted, up and out with the box slung over my arm to stride north along Highway 61. This must be the affluent side of town, the road lined with impressive, detached houses, far larger than the single-storey shacks on the other side. After a couple of miles these mini temples to Mammon give way to open fields of neatly cut grass and well-kept trees.

There is a very little traffic on the road so I notice when a black SUV slows right down as it passes me. It stops up ahead and turns around, passing a second time on the other side only to turn around once more. Tyres screech as it stops, both front doors springing open, two men leaping out. They wear dark suits and wraparound sunglasses. One of them shows me some sort of ID badge. 'Cornelius Parker?' he says. 'I'm Special Agent Bradley from the Department of Homeland Security. That's Special Agent

Smith.' He nods at the other man who, I'm startled to see, has drawn a snub nosed handgun. 'Please put down your bags and hold up your hands,' says Bradley.

'What is this?'

'Do as he says!' orders Smith. He's pointing the gun straight at me.

Bradley bends down to inspect the casket. It's obvious this must be what they are looking for. As he unclasps it, the other agent moves forward and I notice he's no longer focused on me: both men are staring at the heart.

It's hard to explain what happens next but I find it very easy to knock Smith's gun arm out of the way with a sudden motion from my left hand. He drops the weapon as my right hand forms a fist that connects with his face. He tumbles backwards; I turn around. Bradley sees what's happening; he's reaching for his gun but I kick him in the stomach. Truly, the vengeance of the Lord is mine. I pick up the fallen pistol. Bradley is clutching his stomach but with his other hand he's raising his gun. I squeeze the trigger three times and Bradley rolls over. I turn around. The other agent is holding his face. 'Don't do it, please...' I shoot him once, between the eyes.

They're dead. I've killed them. The shots linger loud in my ears.

Two bodies lie still and twisted, blood pooling around them, a stench in the air, the stench of the horsemen. I look this way and that. Have any cars passed? It's so quiet out here. Someone must have heard the gunfire. I think about dropping the pistol then decide to take it with me. I pace forwards and back wondering if I've still got time to try and hide the bodies. Perhaps I should put them back in the SUV? Oh, no, this is crazy. If there are two agents here, there must be more around, ready to pounce. I collect the casket and hurry from the road, running into the trees as fast as I can. Give me wings Jesus, I pray, give me wings that I may fly.

THE ARCHON INVASION

'Professor Jason Carter carefully lowered the rope ladder into the hole.

– Are you sure you're up for this? he asked Anna.

Anna Meridian flinched as the strong wind blew across the dusty Dakota plain. Her eyes shone and her crimson hair shook. – Of course I'm ready, she said. I didn't come through all this just to back out now.

– I love you. The professor turned his handsome face to the wilderness. You're so amazing, and he kissed her passionately on the lips.

– I love you too.'

I take a moment to look up from my book and around the tent. Whenever I read this bit aloud the dialogue always strikes me as way too cheesy and I'm aware I use the adjective 'handsome' too often when describing Professor Carter. The audience continues to watch me. I clear my throat and continue.

'With Professor Carter taking the lead, the couple climbed down the rope ladder into the gaping darkness of the hole. As they made their descent, Anna noticed how the sides of the hole were unusually smooth, as if blasted clean by some sort of laser. With each downward step taking her further and further into the dark, Anna couldn't help but remember the town they had passed through, its empty streets almost swallowed up by the strange, red dust. She remembered the eerie dance of lights in the sky last night, curious shades of yellow and green that she had never quite seen before and the man in the motel with the marks on his neck and eyes like gravestones. They had come so far since the first sightings and rumours, since the government denials and the military takeover, since they discovered the ancient manuscript in the Library of Congress and realised all this to be the fulfilment of a five-thousand-year-old prophecy.

Trembling, now, Anna reached the end of the ladder and dropped the last couple of feet to the bottom of the hole. Carter caught her as she landed, his strong arms keeping her upright. Again, he kissed her. – You're so amazing, he said. But really, she thought, he was the amazing one: he was so intelligent, handsome and brave. Of course, Anna knew that their love was forbidden – she, a PhD student and Carter, her thesis supervisor – but there had been no way to deny the attraction sizzling between them. Anyway, if they were lucky enough to survive this ordeal, the university was certain to reinstate Carter – what they had discovered was too important, more important by far than any qualms the authorities could have about their all-consuming love.

– Will you look at this? Carter aimed his flashlight around the interior of the cavern. The walls shone strangely, the light revealing glinting, gleaming patterns everywhere, swirls and haloes of tightly carved, delicate lines that reminded Anna of nothing more intimate and familiar than her own fingerprints. And there, in the darkest shadows of the hole, she could see part of a gleaming metal structure, like a giant tube or cylinder half submerged, half raised out of the red earth.

– This is it, whispered Carter, the nest of the Nephilim, the layer of the Archon. The manuscript was right all along. We're finally here.

Anna felt it, the waves of dread and evil clinging to the clammy underground air like psychic pollution. Her mind clouded with visions of black-winged birds blocking out the sun. She heard the man who was her supervisor, her lover and her guide gasp in amazement and horror –and she could see it too, something waiting in the darkest depths of the shadows, a terrible evil more ancient than man, more ancient even than the earth itself.'

I finish reading and look up again. A moment of silence in the 'Barclays Wealth' tent before the audience realises I've finished, then a ripple of applause. I'm slightly overwhelmed to see so many people. A good portion of the audience are teenage girls, which isn't surprising (my editor calls them my 'key demographic') but there are all sorts of others as well – even a few men. Alicia, my publicist, said that festival organisers had moved me from the much smaller 'Green Energy' tent where I was originally scheduled to read due to 'unexpected demand'. She's sitting in the front row and stops checking her phone long enough to give me an enthusiastic thumbs-up. I glance across at the host, a jolly fifty-something woman whose name I realise I've already forgotten. Suzy something? Whatshername takes off her glasses and says, 'Wasn't that thrilling everyone? Give Esther Daniels another round of applause.' The audience dutifully oblige. 'We have about ten minutes for questions before moving over to the bookstore for signings.'

At least a dozen hands shoot up.

'Over there,' says Suzy whatshername.

A young woman with a festival T-shirt and a microphone moves through the throng, passing it to a pretty woman in her mid-twenties. 'Hi!' the pretty woman begins. 'I just wanted…' There's a moment of feedback. 'I just wanted to say how much I loved *The Archon Invasion*, it blew my mind.'

'Oh, well, that's really nice of you to say so, thank you,' I hear myself say.

'I just wondered where you get your ideas from?'

'I don't know,' I give a nervous laugh and feel myself redden. How many times have I been asked this question? 'I guess I have an overactive imagination and well, I suppose my life has been quite strange. It still is strange!' I hate myself for laughing again, a stupid girly giggle at the end of the sentence that makes me blush all the more. Oh life!

The next question comes from a skinny guy with a hipster beard and large glasses that magnify his rather dozy brown eyes. 'You said that your life has been a bit strange. Is it true that you were kidnapped by a cult a few years ago?'

I take a sip of water. Alicia catches my eye and nods enthusiastically. I know they want me to talk about this. My British publishers are almost as excited as the Americans about what happened. After I finish the sequel to *The Archon Invasion* my agent is pushing me to write a memoir. 'I think kidnapping would be going a little too far.' The audience watch with me fascination. I'm still a freak, I think, still the odd one out. How am I meant to explain what it was like? It's almost too much to put into words. I keep reminding myself I'm in England – no, Wales, which is different again – but it's all so far removed from White Pines, Earl Landis, the Reverend Parker and all that madness it almost seems like another planet. The thought of putting what happened in a book rather terrifies me. 'When I was fifteen my mother left my dad and took me to live with some, well... I don't know what you'd call them over here. Survivalists maybe? Do you have them here?' From the blank looks I guess not. 'Well, they had a lot of guns and stuff and they didn't like to pay tax or anything like that, um, but well, you know, they believed in all sorts of crazy things as well, like the federal government was in league with aliens and vampires, that the president was the anti-Christ and the end of the world was about to happen. But, as we can see...' and I gesture at the audience as if to say, look, the world hasn't ended. Not yet, anyway. The audience laughs. 'There were some quite strange people in the camp. My mother was one of them.' More laughter. 'At the time it was quite an uncomfortable experience, you know, it was scary but I guess it inspired me, in a way.'

The next question comes from a young woman at the front wearing a headscarf and a 'Free Palestine' T-shirt. 'Esther, you're such an inspiration to me. I really relate to Anna Meridian. Did you intend her to be a strong role model?'

After the questions I say a quick thank you to Suzy-whatshername before Alicia ushers me from the Barclays

Wealth tent to the bookstore tent. 'I've been live tweeting your reading. When are you going to get on Twitter?'

'Soon,' I tell her although I can't think of anything worse.

Outside it's actually raining even harder than earlier and we flinch against the deluge, Alicia opening an umbrella for us. 'It always rains at Hay,' she says, still cheerful and I think it's true, what people told me about coming here, that the Brits just love to talk about the weather. Mind you, I'm not surprised. It was sweltering when I arrived in London two days ago and now it feels like winter has come early.

Alicia leads me into the bookstore tent. A small area has been set aside with a chair and a table piled high with copies of *The Archon Invasion*. The queue already stretches outside. 'You were marvellous,' Alicia squeezes my arm. 'Will you be all right here for a few minutes? I've got to go to the authors' yurt and make sure the Mayor of London has arrived. He's written a new book about Shakespeare, it's tremendously exciting.'

'Okay, great.'

About two hundred people are in the queue and when the last one has left my signature is shot to pieces and my voice is failing. I remember practising my signature in my publisher's offices in New York before the book came out. It was quite elaborate and pretty back then. I used to pride myself on my handwriting – but it's all gone to pieces now, less a signature, more like wild scrawl defacing the title page. The fans seem happy enough though. 'My fans.' I have fans. No boyfriend (well, unless I count Josh back in Brooklyn, but I'm beginning to think he really is the douche people say he is), but plenty of fans. In the bad days back in Orlando I never imagined anything like this would ever happen to me. It's good, I know, but all the same I'm shattered after talking to and seeing so many people, having to 'perform', having to 'be' Esther Daniels 'internationally bestselling author'. It feels good to slip away once the last of the queue has gone and before anyone catches me. Outside I'm just another twenty-two-year-old who likes books. Ignoring the rain, I wander back to the authors' yurt. I want to be alone, but it's too wet for a walk along the river.

The yurt is full of writers and publishing people. I stand at the back, feeling horribly self-conscious and unsure where to sit or what to do. One woman at the signing who was there with her two teenaged daughters kept telling me how 'amazing' I am, such an 'inspiration', such a 'role model'. *As if.* I can't help but contrast her reaction with my mom. There's the letter she sent me from the SuperMax prison after *Invasion* was published. I wish I could banish her words. *'I thought you'd done everything you possibly could to hurt and betray me but then you go and do this, you let Satan guide your pen and you write this vile, devilish book, spreading the devil's message even as you pretend to scorn him. It's like you stuck a dagger through my heart.'* She went on in this fashion for pages. *A dagger through my heart.* Almost funny that Mom should use such a phrase, unconsciously casting herself as the vampire that has to be slain. Perhaps that's what I've been trying to do all these years, slay my mom.

Last night my publishers put me up with a local writer, Tom and his wife and children. They live in a cute cottage on a hillside a few miles away, all very quaint and it would have been nice, I suppose, or nicer – anyway – if not for the rain that seemed to arrive the moment I did. Tom was out but his wife Felicity was very hospitable and we drank tea in the kitchen and talked about Florida – where she had once been on holiday – while their two small children played on the floor. Felicity told me 'Tom was out walking the hills' which, as he explained over dinner, was research for his next book, 'an attempt to trace the relationship between landscape and memory, history and desire'.

He and Felicity were a little baffled when I told them I wrote what my publisher called 'young adult fantasy' and Tom said, 'Oh, like Harry Potter, right? I guess our kids will be into that soon.' I sensed that he was a little dismayed by this prospect, but when I said my book was more to do with UFOs and vampires he embarked on a long story about a farm at the top of the valley where fifty years ago the whole family disappeared in the middle of winter. 'The farmer, his wife and their three children, all gone. The uncanny thing, you see, is that the police found their footsteps in the snow which went out to the top field and then just stopped. No more footprints, nothing. I've never seen anything unusual myself, but this area is notorious for UFO sightings.'

Later, I lay awake in the small guest bedroom, restless and apprehensive. Jet lag, I suppose and anxiety, perhaps, about the event today but my mind often turns back to the events of five years ago at White Pines. My therapist suggested that writing about it – as I suppose I did with *The Archon Invasion* – might help me to achieve what she calls 'closure', but I'm not sure if it does anything other than keep the old wounds opens.

I think back to the morning when the Reverend Parker returned to White Pines. Mom and I had been at the compound for about a month and I had almost got used to sleeping in the tent when I was woken by shouting. I remember peering through the tent flaps to see this strange man running about the compound. He looked like an old hobo in a filthy suit with a massive shaggy beard matted and clogged together and he was banging on the door of Earl's trailer. Earl had been telling us how 'Parker' was due back 'any day now', but I had never expected him to be quite like this: he made enough noise to rouse the entire compound. Earl came tumbling out, topless and pulling on his trousers, Parker striking him while bellowing, 'You fool,' and making him kneel down in the yard. Mom emerged moments later in a frilly pink nightie, her hair a mess, Sue coming after in T-shirt and sweatpants. Behind came Betty with five or six of the kids. They all slept in one big room at the back of Earl's trailer: Mom, his 'wives' and various children. Only Earl kept himself apart, a curtain separating his private bed from the communal space. Sometimes he slept there with Mom, sometimes with Sue, sometimes perhaps both. Even now I dread to think what might have gone on. In any case, I was better off alone in the tent.

All this commotion woke the others: Rawlins and Sarah came out of their trailer, Frank from the shack where he squatted with Pops. In fact, Pops was the only one not to end up kneeling in the dirt while Parker marched backwards and forwards like a demented mannequin screaming at them. The children weren't let off: Parker had them with the others, on their knees scared and crying. Then he saw me in the tent. Although he was a small man, Parker radiated a sort of tight wound manic energy. Bristling like a cactus in the wind, he gestured at me, 'Get out girl, get over here!'

I crawled out of the tent and stood in front of him: I remember I felt suddenly very guilty, as if I was the one who had done something wrong. 'I been observing you!' he shouted at me. 'I been observing you all. Me and the Lord, we watch you, we see your every move.' He held up his index finger. 'I been out in the woods, out in God's bosom, living like the first Adam and I seen you. I know what you do!' He grabbed the hoodie I was wearing and pulled me forward: I was shocked – this man was assaulting me – but none of the others did anything, they all just stayed on their knees, watching. Even my mother! She just sat looking on in judgement as if I was the one in the wrong, as if I deserved this.

None of these are happy memories: Parker dragging me through the wet grass shouting that I was the 'serpent in their midst', the 'unbeliever' the 'demoniacal slut'! Then he turned his attention to Earl, haranguing him for letting Mom and me into the compound. Earl kept trying to say Mom was a 'prophet' and that I was 'cool' but Parker wasn't having it. I had come to realise that Earl, despite all his firearms, his blog and his paranoid stance towards the government was quite a mellow guy, fairly diplomatic and easy going. Unlike Frank he'd never properly been in the military – just the National Guard reserves – and unlike Rawlins I don't think he was a violent man. I guess he had a comfy set-up, loafing about in the compound with his three 'wives' eating barbecue and drinking beer all day thanks to the donations his blog attracted from likeminded people across the States. When he got bored with eating or fucking Mom he would go into the woods with Frank and Rawlins to 'shoot stuff'. He was basically a big dumb idiot and for all his talk I'd come to the conclusion that with him in charge we were never going to go to North Dakota or launch an insurgency against the federal government or do anything. He just wanted to hang out and for everyone in the compound to get along. Now he's doing forty years in a SuperMax so I guess the Department of Homeland Security saw things differently... Anyway, Parker was pissed at Earl, cussing him out for his low morals and his laziness and claiming he had fallen far from God's ways.

Midway through his diatribe Parker stopped, raised his arms and tilted his head to the sky. 'Oh Lord, now I understand...' and he started to rant about how this was God's punishment for leaving his flock. 'I can no more be angry at them, can I Lord, than a shepherd who absconds in the night only to discover on his return that his sheep are on the very edge of a precipice? They don't know what they are doing. They are just sheep.' On and on he went like this until he started to weep: I wondered if that was his 'thing', Holy weeping, like the way Mom always ended at the 'Holy puking' stage when she was all fired up by the Lord. We were there on our knees in the mud watching him rub his eyes and tug at his beard, pleading with God to 'forgive him', to show us 'mercy' and grace us with a 'sign'.

'Excuse me?'

The question breaks my reverie and I look up. It comes from a gentleman, tall, dark and rather handsome I suppose, handsome enough for me to blush – but what am I saying? Everything makes me blush. There's a thin white scar on the left side of the man's cheek but when I look into his rather lovely blue eyes the scar just adds to his rugged, dashing appearance. I guess he's about forty-five and there are a few distinguished streaks of grey in his black hair, but he looks like he's in good shape and he's much better dressed than most of the other people in the yurt, with a perfectly creased blue suit and shoes as polished as black mirrors. 'I don't suppose you could get me some tea, could you?' His voice is so posh – he sounds like the sort of Brit we see on TV – and then I realise he thinks I'm festival staff, one of the interns who hang about doing things like directing authors to the right tent. 'Oh! I don't work here. Sorry.'

'You don't?'

My face is burning. Is it possible to turn any more red? Say it, I tell myself. Tell him what you are. 'I'm an author. Esther Daniels. I know I look young – I am young.'

'An author! Good Lord! I see! I'm very sorry. My mistake. How embarrassing.' It's his turn to blush.

'I know I don't look like an author.'

'No and you're an American too.'

'I am.'

'Esther Daniels? Why do I know that name? Should I have heard of you?'

'Probably not. I wrote a book called *The Archon Invasion*.'

The man takes a step back, shocked. 'Good Lord. You're Esther Daniels? I didn't realise you were on the programme. My daughter Katie loves that book. You're really the author? That's wonderful. Hasn't it done awfully well?'

'Uh-huh.' My face is definitely going to explode.

'I don't suppose you have a copy do you? I'll get it signed for her. She'll be thrilled I met you.'

'Oh, right.' I fumble about. Do I have a copy? Only the one I read from. I guess that will have to do. 'Who shall I make it out to?'

'Katie Masters, if you can.'

My handwriting hasn't much recovered from the sign-a-thon, so I manage an only semi-appalling signature. I pass it to the man who smiles at me and offers his hand, 'Patrick Masters, delighted to meet you.' He has a firm grip and there are calluses on his palm. I'm embarrassed at how sweaty I must be. 'So you're here as an author. Have you had your event yet?'

'Just now.'

'How did it go?'

'Good, I think. There were a lot of people. My wrist aches from signing so many books.'

'That must be good. I'm on soon.'

'Which tent?'

'Barclays Wealth.'

'Snap. So was I! It's the big one.' He must be quite successful, this guy. I'm curious. 'What's um... what do you write about?'

'Do you know the Pathfinder Series?' I look blank. 'Probably not your sort of thing – they're adventure stories about the SAS, you know, British Special Forces, like your Navy SEALS.'

'Oh yeah, right.'

'I'm on my fifth, *Treacherous Waters* about pirates in Somalia. It's a very "now" topic, Somali pirates, or at least that's what my agent said last year when I wrote the bloody thing.' He lowers his voice and leans towards me, 'Of course it's the sort of book all the literary snobs here don't like. In fact, they don't take me seriously at all. They probably don't take you seriously either.' He looks around conspiratorially. 'Don't tell anyone, but the truth is we sell, you know, you and I, our sort of thing sells. It's a fact. That's why we're here. And I don't know about you but it's not rubbish, what I write. A good story and plenty of action – that's what people want – however, I do like to think my novels have a bit more depth and finesse than say, Andy McNab.'

'Right, yes.' I decide not to ask who that is.

'Of course,' Patrick continues, warming to his theme, 'they like the fact I was a captain in the SAS and that I draw on personal experience. And unlike some people I don't use a ghostwriter or anything. Before Sandhurst I read English at Cambridge, you know, some people forget that. They think we're all dumb solders but I've heard more wisdom from the mouth of a sergeant major pinned down under Taliban fire than I ever did from my old tutors.'

'Oh.'

'Anyway, listen to me, banging on—'

'—It's fine.'

'I get a little nervous before these things, would you believe? I saw action in Afghanistan and here I am nervous about speaking at Hay. Ridiculous, I know.'

'No, I totally get you. I was terrified before I went on,' I say, which is true. The man has a wedding ring but then I wonder why I even noticed it. I bet I'm closer to his daughter's age. Must be jet lag.

'Are you all right?'

'Tired, I think. It's a long way from New York.'

'Isn't that the truth? Here, allow me to get us some of that tea I asked for.'

Patrick walks over to the far corner of the tent where there is a buffet of sandwiches and snacks. A quick look round while he's gone. The yurt is bustling with a mixture of people: there are the *writers*, mostly middle-aged men in slightly shabby jackets or similarly-aged women. It's harder to see a common trend with the women but large necklaces, flowery scarves and glasses are very much in. Mingled among them are various publishing people, vivacious, pretty women in their twenties wielding Kindles and iPhones, older editor types whose faintly academic air does not stop them from still looking a lot smarter than the writers they publish. I feel bad that I hardly know who anyone else is. This morning, when Alicia took me to the yurt, I saw Madison Parker Lee – or Trixxxie Foxxx as she used to be called – once the world's most famous pornstar now modestly dressed in an androgynous black suit. Alicia said she was here to promote her memoir *F*ck and Tell* about her time making black and reds for *YouthTube*. Madison waltzed past me as slow and steady as a sphinx padding through the desert, a cold gaze cast in my direction. I don't think she saw me, not really: I was just part of the furniture, but there was a quality to her face, a combination of luminous beauty and an icy sort of absence, as if she was and wasn't really here. Or as if she was here, but in a way that is too intense for the rest of the world to register or fully understand. It was hard to connect her, so sealed and immaculate, to the things she used to do in those films but perhaps that was why she was so successful? I've seen a few of her black and reds. Everyone has. I think I read that she's still the most watched woman on the Internet. But there's no sign of her here anymore.

Patrick returns with a tray, two cups and a teapot. 'Here we go.' The warm tea is welcome. 'When are you going back to the States?'

'Um...' I take a minute. 'The day after tomorrow. A car is taking me to London tonight. I'm doing an event in a bookstore tomorrow evening. Then back to New York.'

'Is that where you live?'

'Um... sort of. Yeah. Well I rent this place in Brooklyn. It's not much and it's Brooklyn...'

'It's hip there, right?' My awkwardness seems to amuse him.

'I guess.'

'You're hip. No?'

'Me? I don't think so.'

'Oh come on, you're hipper than me.'

'You don't need to be hip. You were in the special forces.'

'That's true.'

'What does hip even mean anyway?'

'You're asking me? I remember when a hipster was originally about jazz.'

'It was?'

'I think so.'

'Yeah, I think I knew that.' I'm smiling at him. Well, this is weirdly fun. Me and Patrick, having tea and chatting away. I realise I don't really like talking about Brooklyn. In so many ways it seems to be a ridiculous place. 'I've never been here before.'

'Hay?'

'All of it. Hay, England, Wales.'

'Goodness. Well, I hope you had a chance to pop into Hay?'

'I walked around for half an hour this morning, that's all.'

'You know most towns round here aren't like that, don't you? Not so many second-hand bookshops.'

'I bet. It was so quaint! Do you live in London?'

'Once upon a time. I'm out in Hampshire now. We have a cottage. I imagine you would describe it as quaint. After three tours of duty I just want a quiet life.'

'I bet.' Christ, stop saying that! I sound like an idiot. 'I know the feeling.' Even worse! I talk more to try and cover myself. 'Some crazy things happened to me when I was growing up and this sort of feels like another of them, you know? Being here, having a bestselling novel, coming to England to promote it. It's crazy. When I was younger I never went anywhere.'

'No?'

'Literally. I was fifteen before I ever left Florida and that was because my mom wanted to join this crazy cult.'

'Extraordinary. I can see that I was wrong about you.'

'When I was young I always wanted to go and live in Norway.'

'I suppose it might happen. Although, mind you, the Norwegian book market is quite small. Have you read that guy Knausgaard people have been going on about? He's Norwegian.'

Knaus-who? Someone else I'm embarrassed to realise I've never heard of. 'No, but... I mean, I don't follow it all that closely.'

'It? It's not a football team!'

Why does this dashing man find me so amusing? 'Right. Sorry.' Oh God. *Life*!

Patrick doesn't notice my humiliation. 'Apparently one in three Norwegians have read his books! One in three. Can you imagine? But I suppose there are only about three million of them. Still, he's a big deal. I read the first one, all about his father dying. I didn't get it really. It's sort of grim and nothing happens.'

'Nothing?'

'Well his father dies and he spends about two hundred pages cleaning out his old house. It was rather depressing.'

'Do you think that was the point?'

'Who knows? Norway. Perhaps I just don't get it.' He takes a sip of tea and smiles as if to suggest it's all a bit of a joke. 'You could live there though.'

'Maybe I will.'

'What about your parents? They must be very proud.'

If only. I make a snorting noise. 'We don't get on. They're very religious, they don't approve of writing books or of any book that isn't the Bible, in fact.'

'How positively awful.'

'Plus my mom is doing a twenty-year term, no parole, so it's not like I see her much anyway.'

'Good Lord. Jail?'

'Uh-huh.'

'Very religious and a convict. How extraordinary. Dare I ask why she's inside?'

'You'll never believe me.'

'Go on.'

'She was convicted of conspiring to bring down the federal government.'

'And there I was thinking you were a girl who served tea. It just goes to show you never can tell.'

'Don't judge a book by its cover right?'

'Right. That must be hard on you though. What about your father?'

'—He's useless,' I cut in. 'He's still down in Florida.' He doesn't go to church so much anymore, I want to add. Without his faith he takes a lot of meds, watches a lot of TV. It might be better if he still went to church.

'Extraordinary. You should write about this.'

Yeah? Like perhaps when my father dies I'll end up writing a book about clearing out all his old stuff like this Knausgaard person. 'My agent said the same thing.'

'Listen to your agent. That's the advice my agent always gives me, anyway,' Patrick bursts out laughing. 'Anyway, look at the time. I'm on in five minutes. Better go for a wee. It was jolly lovely to meet you.'

'Yes.' It *is* possible to blush more, I realise. My cheeks are like blowtorches.

He holds my gaze. There's something quite compelling about the scar on his cheek. I want to ask if it's a war injury or if it was caused by something quite ordinary. I rub my wrist and for a moment imagine what it might be like to touch his scar. He says, 'You're not around later are you? We could get dinner. There's a nice pub I know.'

'Oh! Gosh.' What was that? Dinner? What, with me? Was that a pass? Is he making a pass at me? What does he think? 'I've got to get back to London,' I babble, 'the publishers sent a car.'

'Of course, of course, I forgot, I'm sorry, you've got that thing tomorrow.'

'I'm sorry. It would have been great.'

What am I saying? 'Indeed, it would have been great. Lovely to meet you, Esther.' Patrick smiles again, but with less intensity than before, as if to wipe away whatever implication might have lurked behind his invitation. He holds up his copy of *The Archon Invasion*, 'My daughter will be so thrilled to have this, thank you.' He leans forward for a quick goodbye kiss, his rough cheek brushing against mine, one hand briefly touching my arm. I smell expensive cologne, a slightly woody odour that I remember for days after without ever quite deciding whether I like it or not.

'Good luck with the event!' He exits the yurt.

I realise I'm in a fluster. For a moment I regret my hesitancy. Perhaps I could change my plans, ask Alicia if the car could come tomorrow? I could sneak into Patrick's reading and then we could go for dinner and then... but where would I stay? Unless... No, he's married and at least twenty years older than me. I'm being ridiculous. I'm not Anna Meridian and Patrick isn't Professor Carter.

An hour later and I'm in the car. It has finally stopped raining, but thick grey clouds swallow the surrounding hills and reach all the way down to earth like great devouring worms. We whisk through small villages, cute houses crammed together, bunting strung between modest stone churches and pubs. Everywhere looks closed and as I sit waves of fatigue, sadness and regret threaten to overwhelm me. Jet lag. I know that if none of this had happened, if Mom never met Earl, if Dad never committed the 'incident' at Disney World I'd probably still be in Orlando, I wouldn't be an 'internationally bestselling author' or 'young adult fiction sensation' being driven from Hay-on-Wye to London.

Now we're on the highway. The steady monotony of traffic. Almost dark and there's little to see. The driver doesn't talk and that's fine, I don't feel like talking either. I've talked enough for today. Parker talked a lot. He never stopped. That crazy, sick man. After he had us all kneeling in the dirt weeping, praying and singing in a continuous, frantic performance he took Earl and the two of them went off into the woods for a long time. A strange calm descended over the compound broken only once by a single, blood-curdling scream. I think it was Earl. I remember Mom, the sheen of concern that coloured her face. Soon enough the two returned, and we could all tell that something had happened. I don't know what Parker said or did to Earl in the woods but Earl looked like a man whose soul had been harrowed, as if he'd been opened up, peeled apart and put together quite differently. He spoke quite calmly, his voice flat and dry as he told us all to line up outside his trailer. The day was hot and humid, I remember, and it started to rain, drops the size of little fists falling from the bruised sky, the odd distant flash and boom of the approaching storm, the wind in the trees, a great rustling and hissing. We were stood there as Parker took this thing out of a box. 'Behold,' he exclaimed, holding it aloft, 'the heart of a demon.'

It was at this point I realised we really were in the company of a complete lunatic. I don't know what it was, this thing, like maybe the dried-out heart of a bull or an ox, but Parker exclaimed, 'Brethren, with this we shall work miracles. We shall start a mighty revival such as the world has never seen. With our righteous blood we shall cleanse this heart and birth a seraphim. Then the world shall know that these are indeed the last days and times, that the end is nigh and Christ will return with a mighty sword to judge the wicked and redeem the righteous.' He said something like that, anyway, I don't recall his exact words. But I do remember watching – we all watched – as Parker took Earl's bare arm and held it over the heart. Then, withdrawing a large knife from his grimy suit he made a small cut on Earl's wrist and let the blood trickle over it. As this happened Earl didn't say anything: he was very pale, his eyes bulging with fear. Next, Parker gestured to Rawlins and Frank, repeating the process, cutting their wrists, letting their blood mingle with Earl's over the heart. 'Now the women,' Parker intoned. Mom went first. She seemed almost keen, eagerly offering her wrist, shining with an empty smile on her face as if this moment was the affirmation she had always been looking for. She was drinking more than ever, of course, usually rolling drunk by lunchtime but no one seemed to care or notice. I remember thinking this can't be right, this creature cannot be my mom, but she was, she was my mom. It was horrible. Sarah went next, humming a hymn to herself as the knife broke her skin, as the blood fell, nonchalant as a traveller getting a vaccine. Sue and Betty were more reluctant but Rawlins stood beside us, keeping us in line, a pistol clearly visible sticking out of his pants. Finally, Parker turned his attention to the children. The kids were crying and sobbing, several running away, trying to hide underneath the trailers or broken-down cars. Only Pops stood to one side, ignored by the others. 'You're crazy!' I heard him snarling at Parker, but it didn't make any difference. Pops was good for nothing pretty much all the time. I remember screaming at them to stop, pleading with Parker to show some reason but he seized me, his dirty fingers grabbing my cheeks, his face pressing close to mine: I could smell him, his breath reeking like an open sewer, as if his soul had died within, the rot leaking out, his eyes rolling like marbles, bits of leaves and branches caught in his matted beard, his pale suit soaked yellow with sweat and ooze. Rawlins grabbed my arms and held me fast as Parker cut me: we stood over the heart, my blood dripping down. There was blood everywhere and as Rawlins seemed almost to crush me I felt a strange tugging at the back of my head, between my eyes, my terror opening the world and for weeks after I dreamt of this moment; dreamt of Parker, standing in a shifting red desert, the heart in one hand, a burning sword in the other.

The moment Rawlins released me, I ran blindly into the forest. Three times in the last month I had tried to run away and three times I ended up returning defeated, exhausted, starving and thirsty – the endless woods, the territory beyond somehow too vast, too much in this heat, too far from civilisation – but this time I didn't think of that. I just ran.

I wonder what Patrick would have said if I told him what happened in the woods? How I stumbled blindly in the dark and the rain, covered in mud, cut and torn by branches and brambles until the men leapt out as silent and hidden as living shadows: the gloved hand that covered my mouth and stifled my screams; the other hands that lashed my arms behind my back. Perhaps, if we'd gone to dinner, I could have told Patrick the story of the 'Enhanced Interrogation Facility' where they held me for weeks until I'd explained everything to them a hundred times and they finally realised I wasn't a threat to national security. Because I ran into the woods, because the Department of Homeland Security got me first I missed it. I was already in 'Protective Custody' when the raid took place, when Rawlins was shot dead, when Frank and Sarah were injured and one of the children, eight-year-old Bo, was hit by a stray bullet and left paralysed from the waist down. I wonder if I'd go back from this incident and tell Patrick about the children, how I made friends with them, how we used to pass the time at White Pines playing in the dirt and the trees. They were like me, you see, they didn't choose to be there, shit just happened to them, to us. We all drew the same short straw. At least they're all out of it now, scattered far and wide to foster parents. Apart from poor little Bo.

One person did escape. I learnt later that Parker was wanted for the murder of two federal agents in Arkansas. The killings confirmed federal suspicions about the *OathKeepers* blog. Earl's connection to Parker implicated everyone and they raided us. More than five years later and Parker is still at large, currently number ten on the FBI's 'most wanted' list. I wonder if he's out there now, a ragged man wandering the countryside like a lost prophet of old, still clutching his heart.

As I think I said, the dreams stopped, eventually.

The faint scar left by his blade is still there, on my wrist and I trace it with my fingers. It's almost comforting, the subtle transition to the white, half-moon indentation. Almost. We drive on into the night, I sit back and I think about what could have been.

UNEPILOGUE

Let me try to be clear, this isn't really an epilogue. What is an epilogue anyway – the after-the-end? The summing-up? There will be no summing up here, I'm afraid, no clear or comforting resolution. It's not like anything ends anyway. No, what I want to do is to tell you a bit more about Esther and, I suppose, a little bit more about myself.

I met Esther the evening after her event in Hay. She gave a reading at Waterstones Piccadilly (I wasn't there) and then went on to a drinks reception thing thrown by her publishers. I was at the reception because we had the same publishers – although Esther was on their big, commercial imprint, the one that gets books in airports and places like WHSmith – and I wasn't. The reception was in a converted church near Spitalfields. I'd been in two minds about going because I am, at heart, shy and anti-social but in the end I went. The reception wasn't just for her, it was some sort of anniversary of the publishing house, a big jamboree to which hundreds of people had been invited. I hardly knew anybody and so was hanging around at the back with a glass of water wondering if I should say hello to my editor, who was busy talking to some of the much more famous writers that he also edits. As I said, my second novel hadn't done as well as we hoped and I found myself worrying that if I was not exactly unwelcome (I had been invited, after all) then perhaps... well... I don't know.

Esther was also standing by the wall, more or less next to me. I didn't really notice her until we accidentally made eye contact and then immediately looked away, both of us and then looked back again; she smiled at me, but still, that was nice and I figured, why not say hello? She was perhaps the youngest and least intimidating-looking person in the room – sort of pretty, I suppose, a petite woman with tangled blond-brown hair and large brown eyes, trim legs skinny in tight jeans, her top amorphous in an oversized blue shirt and a long scarf. We started talking and although I'd never heard of her – I'm not much interested in young adult fantasy, have never read *Harry Potter, Hunger Games* or any of that stuff – we bonded over our mutual awkwardness. She said that she'd never been to London before, I waffled on about how great it was blah blah blah. I liked her American accent. I like Americans, I told her, many of my best friends are Americans (this is true). I told her I'd lived in America as a small child (Darien, Connecticut) and that all my first memories were of America – our station wagon with faux wooden side panels, a swing and a tree house in the back yard, thick snow in the winter when it would get so cold that even the sea would start to freeze or else sitting on scorching porch steps in the summer, going to Disney World and up the Empire State, the amazing red and silver fire engines that would go screaming out of the station down the street from our house and that, as a small boy, I found exceptionally thrilling... even the white picket fence we had around the house. All the classic American Dream type tropes.

I'm not sure if Esther was very interested – I was nervous so I talked over her, 'mansplained' excessively, I'm sure, probably went on far too much about 'how to write' when she was the one with the internationally best-selling novel... I mean, honestly, what could I have told her about writing that she wouldn't already know? But I can't have been all bad because when I suggested leaving to get a drink elsewhere she said 'okay' and we slipped out without saying goodbye to anyone. In retrospect, that was probably quite rude but there was something exciting about being so secretive.

We ended up in a bar I knew near Brick Lane that was open late. Things weren't quite as bad for me then as they were when you started this book, but they were still a bit off kilter – I was going through one of my periods of insomnia where I seemed unable to sleep for more than an hour or two. I'd spend much of the day strung-out but would become weirdly animated in the darker hours, knocking around like some restless, over-charged particle. We got quite drunk on not very much and caught a black cab back to her hotel. She had never ridden in one before, I insisted on paying and we kissed in the back and held hands. Esther's hotel turned out to be a Travelodge near King's Cross. I might have thought our publishers would splash out for somewhere a bit smarter as she was a bestselling author and all, but no – she got a Travelodge. A tiny, functional room, a view of nothing but the back of buildings, plumbing and air conditioning vents, the promise of a high-fat breakfast... but at least the bed was comfortable.

I'm not going to tell you what we did or didn't do. This isn't some kiss and tell nonsense. But that night in the bar, later in her bedroom and then over breakfast Esther revealed quite a lot about herself – about her mom and what happened at the camp. I got over my earlier garrulousness and let her talk. I've often found myself to be one of those people that others like to confide in. People tell me things they shouldn't, they confess and reveal secrets. What happened to her wasn't quite the same as I have it here; I changed all the names, used a lot of artistic license. I elaborated, but not as much as you might think. Life is weirder than fiction anyway, filled with synchronicities and coincidences that just wouldn't work in a story. The funny thing is, in some of his stories, 'Tim' had also mentioned this blog, the one Earl (not his real name) kept. The strands connect, it's all part of the same strange scene, a subterranean America full of un-American activities.

After Esther went back to the States, I read her book. In all honesty, I thought it was fairly awful, clichéd nonsense with daft characters, predictable plots, gauche sentimentality – all the stuff I hate in a novel – but then I guess I wasn't the target audience. We kept in touch, off and on – more off than on – by then I was dating someone else and it seemed inappropriate or... well, I don't know... Esther never went on Twitter or Facebook so I wasn't able to keep track of her. She never wrote a memoir either but a sequel followed the first novel and that was followed by another, more successful than the first – she knew how to churn them out (not that I read the sequels) – and since then... well... look, Esther isn't her real name so it's up to you to guess who she is, if you want... but that isn't the point, that's another story. It's not like we have a meaningful plot here anyway, there's no clear trajectory from beginning through middle to crisis and then on to acute crisis – you know, the moment in the story when all seems lost and from where things go on to climax and resolution, the five acts, all that – no, that's not what happens and we all know it's not the way things happen, not in life even if in fiction. But as I tell my students, books or rather 'texts' have nothing to do with life anyway – books are about other books, words are about words and yes, we use them to explain things to ourselves but they never quite match up, stories and reality, stories and life, not really. And perhaps that's for the best.

ACKNOWLEDGEMENTS

I had a lot of fun writing this book, but no book is written alone. I'd like to thank my wonderful agent, Anna Power and the Dodo Ink crew for taking this on. I'd also like to thank Sam Jordison and Eloise Miller at Galley Beggar Press for publishing an earlier version of 'Exploding Zombie Cock' as a Galley Beggar Short. Huge respect is due to all the independent publishers out there, championing risky, good quality new fiction. Previous versions of 'Eat My Face' and 'Hope's End' were published in *Paraphilia Magazine* and the anthology *A Dream of Stone*. Thanks also to Rob Doyle, Tom Bullough, Michael Sayeau and Seraphina Madsen for reading drafts of these pieces and to my parents, for all their support and very few questions. Finally, the most thanks are due to my wife, Lucy Buckroyd, for all her love, kindness and patience.